THE DAGGER OF NEMESIS

A JUDGE MARCUS FLAVIUS SEVERUS MYSTERY IN ANCIENT ROME

ALAN SCRIBNER

Torcular Press

Also by Alan Scribner

Judge Marcus Flavius Severus Mysteries in Ancient Rome
Mars the Avenger
The Cyclops Case
Marcus Aurelius Betrayed
The Return of Spartacus
Mission to Athens
Across the River Styx
The Persian Assassin
A Shipwreck Conspiracy

Anni Ultimi: A Roman Stoic Guide to Retirement,
    Old Age and Death
With J.C. Douglas Marshall

ISBN 13: 9798540916417 (paperback)

Library of Congress Control Number: 2021916876
Amazon Kindle Direct Publishing
Seattle, Washington

Dedication
Ruth and Paul

TABLE OF CONTENTS

SCROLL V 181

PERSONAE

Judge Severus' familia and court personnel
Marcus Flavius Severus – judge in the Court of the Urban Prefect and *iudex selectus*
Artemisia – Severus' wife
Aulus, Flavia, and Quintus, their 22, 20 and 14-year old children
Alexander – Severus' freedman and private secretary
Quintus Proculus – court clerk
Gaius Sempronius Flaccus – judicial assessor
Caius Vulso – centurion in the Urban Cohort
Publius Aelianus Straton – *tessararius* in the Urban Cohort
Crantor of Rhodes – pankratiast and Severus' bodyguard
Scorpus, Tryphon, Glycon, Sarapion -family slaves
Argos – family dog
Phaon – family cat

Persons connected with the case of the murder of the charioteer Zephyrus
Zephyrus – murdered charioteer of the Red faction
Gaius Gordianus – *Dominus* of the Red faction
Paris – friend and sometime lover of Zephyrus
Nicias – assistant to Gordianus

Phlius – groom of Zephyrus' horse Compressor

Persons connected with the case of the murder of the courtesan Atalanta
Atalanta – high priced courtesan
Novatilla – Atalanta's mother
Vipsania – Atalanta's daughter
Gaius Sergianus Heron – Atalanta's bodyguard

Publius Pictor – a painter and former lover of Atalanta
Lucius Manilius Crispinus – a retired general and former lover of Atalanta
Marilla – slave and *ornatrix* of Atalanta

Persons connected with the case of the murder of the shoemaker Pedo
Pedo – shoemaker in the Subura
Lupus – agent for owner of Pedo's apartment house
Septimius Scapula – Propraetor of Bithynia
Quintus Mucius – Scapula's son-in-law and *comes*
Perpetua – wife of Scapula
Septimia – daughter of Scapula
Musa – slave of Scapula
Adebugius – overseer of slaves in the *domus* of Scapula
Lucius Papirius – Pedo's lawyer
Tiberius Sosius Tertullus – Senator and prosecutor of Scapula, Mucius and Pedo
Claudius Glabrio – a tout

Others
Lucius Sergius Paullus – Urban Prefect of the City of Rome
Publius Flamma – army friend of Aulus

The story is set in Rome in the spring and summer of the year 173 CE, 2 years after the events in *A Shipwreck Conspiracy.*

Roman hours: The day was divided into 12 day hours, starting from sunrise and 12 night hours from sunset. The length of the hour and the onset time of the hour depended on the season since there is more daylight in summer, more night in winter. In the spring and fall, close to an equinox, the hours were approximately equal to ours in length, with the 1st hour of the day at 6-7 am and the 1st night hour at 6-7 pm.

The events in this book take place in the spring and summer. In the summer, a day hour can last up to an hour and 15 minutes, while a night hour is correspondingly shorter, 45 minutes.

For simplicity, the equinox times of the hours mentioned in this book are:

1st	hour of the day	– 6 – 7 am
2nd	hour of the day	– 7 – 8 am
3rd	hour of the day	– 8 – 9 am
4th	hour of the day	– 9 – 10 am
5th	hour of the day	–10 – 11 am
9th	hour of the day	– 2 – 3 pm
10th	hour of the day	– 3 – 4 pm
1st	hour of the night	– 6 – 7 pm
2nd	hour of the night	– 7 – 8 pm
3rd	hour of the night	– 8 – 9 pm
5th	hour of the night	–10 – 11 pm
9th	hour of the night	– 2 – 3 am

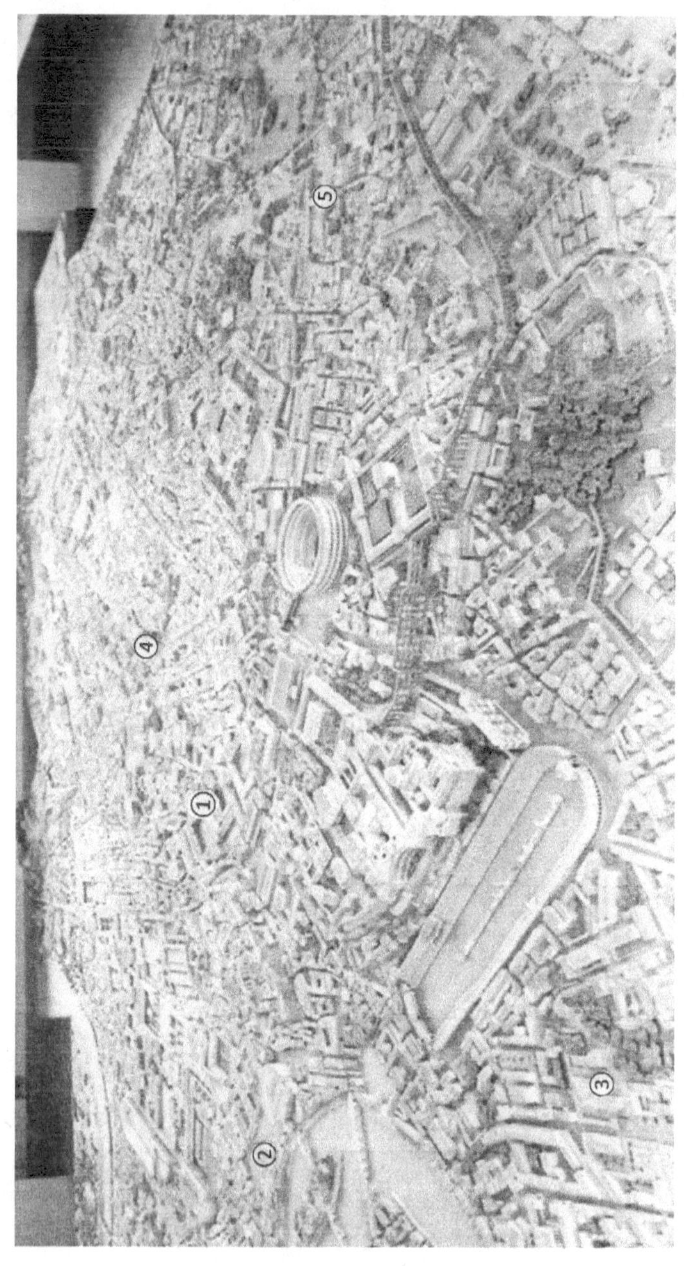

Ancient Rome

The picture on the left shows the model of ancient Rome in the Museum of Roman Civilization in Rome.

The numbers on the picture locate places mentioned in the book, according to the following key.

1. Forum of Augustus, where Judge Severus has his courtroom and chambers.
2. Red faction stables
3. Aventine Hill insula of Atalanta
4. Subura insula of the shoemaker Pedo
5. Severus' luxury *insula* on the Caelian Hill and nearby park

SCROLL I

I

MARCUS FLAVIUS SEVERUS: TO HIMSELF

Seneca once wrote that children play a game of magistrates, imitating the lictors with their *fasces* axe in a bundle of rods, the judge dressed in his reddish-purple bordered toga *praetexta* and the Tribunal. Adults, observed Seneca, played the same game, only in the forums or in the Senate.

I sometimes think that when I come out of retirement to accept a new *cognitio*, I'm just playing games. I may give this reason or that, each of which sounds socially or legally persuasive, but really it's all games. Just as I am a strong player of the board game *latrunculi*, I seem to be a strong player in catching criminals. Hemming in and capturing my opponent's pieces in *latrunculi*, or hemming in and capturing a criminal may be the same thing at bottom. That's the way I felt when I received a personal plea from the Urban Prefect of the City of Rome to help catch a dangerous murderer on the loose before he could kill again. It was when he said 'no one else' that I felt a trap closing in on me.

It started in June, two years after I uncovered the perpetrator of the shipwreck conspiracy. I was again enjoying my retirement in our villa in the Alban hills. I was busy studying astronomy, observing the stars and planets, thinking about what I saw and reading what our philosophers of Nature have thought about the heavens. My 14-year-old son Quintus, unusually gifted in mathematics and geometry, was my companion in these studies. While I was reading Aristotle and Lucretius, he was delving into the astronomical calculations of Aristarchus, Eratosthenes and Ptolemy. And we were discussing everything.

My wife Artemisia was well into her new biography of Aspasia, the learned concubine of Pericles, who Socrates himself had named as the one person able to best him in argument. But she was having problems because she didn't think this book was coming along as well as her previous biography of Cleopatra. I read over what she had written so far and didn't agree with her. I thought this biography was quite as good. She didn't believe me, but was encouraged to press ahead nevertheless.

My 20-year-old daughter Flavia was deeply into her music and poetry, but still grieving over having had to break up with her beloved Bellerephon, who she couldn't marry because he was a slave, though a well-educated, interesting and handsome young man. Still there was no future in marrying a slave except social ostracism for her and illegitimacy for any child they might have. She had promised to stop seeing him, but whether she could keep that promise was not certain. Artemisia and I hoped she would find someone else. That was the only cure, if a cure was possible.

My 22-year-old son Aulus was now with us again, back in Rome on assignment from his legion, XII Fulminata, based in Cappadocia. He was tasked with informing the government in Rome of the situation in Cappadocia, keeping the authorities up to date about what was happening or not happening in that part of the Empire. He was therefore stationed in the Castra Peregrina on the Caelian Hill, not far from our apartment in Rome.

Our dog Argos and cat Phaon were both happy in the country, with plenty of space in the surrounding fields and woods to pursue their dog and cat interests, particularly smaller animals. But now both sensed Flavia's distress. Instead of alternating sleeping spots with various members of the family, as they usually did, both snuggled closer to Flavia every night, Phaon sleeping on her bed, Argos sleeping on the floor beside it. They were a comfort to her.

For me, it was as perfect as life could be.

Then one day in July a messenger arrived announcing that the Urban Prefect, Lucius Sergius Paullus, requested my indulgence for a visit in two days. The purpose was not stated.

I politely welcomed his visit, and offered lunch and a swim in our pool. At the same time, I suspected that this would not be just a friendly convivial visit for him, to exchange news and gossip and spend a day in the country, away from the hot, stifling, overcrowded Urbs. Rather I was sure the Prefect wanted something from me. And what else could that be, but help with an intractable criminal case.

How right I was. There was a mass murderer on the loose in Rome. In three days, he had killed three people and had written a number in blood on the cheek of each of them. On the first victim he wrote the number 'I'. On the second, the number 'II'. On the third 'III'.

I was supposed to find this murderer before there would be a number 'IV'.

II

A VISIT FROM THE
URBAN PREFECT

The Urban Prefect arrived at Severus' villa in a 4-horse *carpentum* coach. He had a secretary and a slave with him and was still dictating instructions even as his vehicle was stopped in front of the entrance to the villa. Needless to say, Severus was informed as the coach was sighted nearing the villa, and came outside with Artemisia and all three of his children. The family's black Molossian dog Argos was always interested in visitors and joined in the welcoming, while their orange Egyptian cat Phaon did not care for visitors and was off on his own somewhere. He would reappear when the visitors left.

Severus was dressed in a formal toga to greet the arrival of the Prefect, a burden in general and even more so on a hot July day. The rest of his family had on lightweight comfortable and stylish tunics, with colorful geometric patterns, except for Aulus who wore his red military tunic and wide military belt. As he descended from his coach, the Urban Prefect was also dressed in a formal toga, while his secretary and slave wore silk tunics. The only difference between the Prefect's attire and Severus' was that Paullus wore a tunic with a broad reddish-purple Senatorial stripe showing from beneath his toga, while Severus had a narrow reddish-purple Equestrian stripe showing from beneath his.

Severus and Paullus exchanged greeting kisses on the lips as was customary between upper class Romans. Paullus made sure to call Severus by his Equestrian title, *eminentissime*, while Severus made sure to use the Senatorial title, *clarissime*, most illustrious, when first greeting the Prefect. Severus then introduced Paullus to his family and the Prefect introduced them to his aides. Then Severus escorted Paullus and his two aides into the villa.

"Please," Severus said right off, departing from the formalities, "take off your toga and we will all be much more comfortable." Without a word the Prefect virtually threw his into the hands of his slave, while Severus handed his to his slave Glycon, who was waiting for them as they came into the house.

"I have refreshments ready in the garden," Severus told the Prefect. "Afterwards I'll show you the villa. First, drinks and snacks. Then lunch. And then a swim in our pool."

"That sounds excellent."

The visitors were led through the house, through the atrium, tablinum and peristyle, and into the garden where a table with white wine and fruit was already set up. They all took seats, including the slaves.

The eight then refreshed themselves with wine and fruit.

"Excellent wine," said the Prefect. "And the grapes are quite tasty. Are they local?"

"They grow right behind the house. The ones on the table were picked this morning. And the wine is a Falernian, as you certainly know."

After some polite chatter about the weather in Rome, hotter and smellier than usual, according to the Prefect, he told his aides that he wanted to discuss a few matters with his host alone. As they rose, Severus' family took the hint and left the garden as well. They escorted the guests to their swimming pool out back, inviting them to join them for a swim.

Then the Prefect got down to business. "Severus, I come to you because I don't know what else to do. We have a murderer at large in Rome who is challenging us in a brutal way. We don't know who he is. We don't know why he's committing these murders or how he chooses his victims. We are stymied. We need help." The Prefect held up his hand to forestall a negative reply he suspected Severus was automatically going to give him, and continued. "I know you're retired from the Court of the Urban Prefect, and I know you don't want to have anything to do with crime anymore. But hear me out first."

Severus shrugged, but was silent, waiting to hear what the Prefect had to say.

"I come to you because of your success in solving crimes no one else can solve. You've proven that for years now, ever since that notorious case of the body found on the steps of the Temple of Mars the Avenger, right through your recent brilliant uncovering of the mastermind behind the shipwreck conspiracy."

"It's not necessary to review these cases, Prefect," interrupted Severus, who didn't care for flattery, even if true.

"All right. This murderer has already killed three people and left a calling card each time. Each time he wrote a number in his victim's blood on his dead victim's cheek. I, II, and III for each victim successively. We don't want there to be a IV or a V or a VI."

"Writing a number in the blood of the victim on the victim's face is really sinister. Even more so if he dipped his finger in his victim's blood to write it, as seems likely. Tell me about the victims. Who were they, how were they killed, when did it happen and where?"

"The first victim was a chariot driver. Zephyrus."

"Zephyrus, the charioteer for the Reds?"

"You've heard about it?"

"I heard that he died. But the Daily Acts, I heard, reported his death as the result of a chariot crash. I didn't know he was murdered."

"We couldn't put the truth on the news boards of the Daily Acts in the Old Forum. If the fans of the Reds knew Zephyrus had been murdered, they would jump to the conclusion that someone from the Blues, or Greens or Whites was responsible and might seek revenge. Their charioteers would then be at risk. You know how volatile Roman sports fans can be."

"Yes. I do. I myself was a serious fan of the Reds when I was growing up because the great Diocles was driving for them then. And I still take an interest in the Reds, though it's more casual now, since I live in the country and don't get to the chariot races any more. Also, I have a lot of other interests. But tell me what happened."

"One night a month ago, two days before the Kalends of May, Zephyrus was at a banquet at the Red faction stables when he received a message tablet and quickly left. Later that night he was found dead in an alley on the Aventine Hill. His throat had been cut and the number 'I' had been written on his cheek in blood, probably his own blood.

"We, that is, the *Vigiles* and the Urban Cohort, investigated the case but found nothing. No one seemed to have anything against Zephyrus, except maybe for the Blues, Greens and Whites who competed with him in the Circus. But that is just a sporting rivalry. Not cause for murder. At least I don't think so."

"Who was the second victim?"

"She was a famous courtesan in her day. But now older and retired, though when she was murdered last month, I'm told, she was still beautiful and desirable. She lived on the Aventine Hill. Her name is Atalanta, like the virgin huntress of myth. Perhaps this one was a huntress, but obviously not a virgin."

The name caught Severus up short. He knew Atalanta. It was when he turned 16 years of age. It was the night he first put on his *toga virilis*, his formal initiation from boy to man. His father's present was a night with one of the most beautiful and accomplished courtesans of the day. That was Atalanta. That was the night he graduated from casual inexperienced assignations with slaves or brothel 'she-wolves' into knowledge of the arts of love. He had been nervous, but Atalanta calmed him, then tendered to him. She played the lyre for him, sang to him, conversed charmingly and intelligently with him. In short, she seduced him. Then she brought out passion and lust and taught him about both. Even now, 35 years later, he was still smitten by the memory of that night. And now Atalanta was dead. Murdered.

The Prefect noticed a faraway look had come into Severus' eyes. "Did you know her?"

"It was a long time ago," replied Severus. "But yes, I knew Atalanta. Tell me what happened?"

"It was like the case of the chariot driver. She was at a dinner party with her mother and her daughter and some guests. She received a message tablet and left. She had a personal bodyguard but she told him to stay home. Later, she was found murdered, her throat cut, and the number II written on her cheek in blood."

"How long after the murder of the Zephyrus was Atalanta murdered?"

"The next day, actually. On the day before the Kalends of May. She was found dead in an alley on the Aventine Hill, not far from the alley where Zephyrus was found."

"And the third?"

"The third was a nobody. A common shoemaker who lived in the Subura. His name was Pedo."

"Just Pedo? Not three names like a Roman citizen or two names like a normal person."

"As far as I know, his name was Pedo. Just Pedo. He was a recluse. No wife, no concubine, nobody seemed to know him at all. His throat was also cut. He was killed in the back of his shoe shop, we think on the Kalends of May, the day after Atalanta was murdered and two days after the murder of Zephyrus. But we don't know for sure because his body wasn't found until a few days after he was killed. The number III was written on Pedo's cheek in his blood."

"So it looks like Zephyrus and Atalanta were killed in alleys on the Aventine Hill, but Pedo was killed in his room in the Subura."

The Prefect nodded yes.

"And you want me to catch the criminal before there's a number IV?"

"That's what I'm hoping."

Severus gave a doubtful look. "First, it seems that this was a murder spree with three victims, one after the other, one day after another. So there may not be a fourth. If there were, why wasn't it done the day after the murder of Pedo?"

The Prefect shrugged. "I have no idea. All I know is that we are stymied." The Prefect thought for a moment. "If you're to take on this *cognitio*, as I hope you will, I suppose I should tell you the primary reason why I'm asking your help. It's that I am under great pressure to solve this case and the pressure is not just from the Red faction, but from all the racing factions. If a Red charioteer was murdered by someone from any of the other racing factions, the Reds will want revenge. And while they have put it out so far that Zephyrus' death was an accident, that's just provisional. The Reds need to know who killed him, as do the Greens, Blues and Whites, so I need this case solved before things break out of control. The Reds are pressuring me harder all the time. I can't take this sort of pressure much longer.

I need a solution and the *Vigiles* and my Urban Cohort are not able to produce one."

"I understand. But I can't confine any investigation solely to the case of the charioteer. After all, there were three people killed in three days. And all with the same *modus operandi*. These deaths must be connected. Do you know anything the three victims had in common? Do you have any motive? Do you know even one detail about the criminal?"

The Prefect shook his head negatively.

Severus gave back a doubtful look. "Let me talk to my wife. Meanwhile, my son Aulus will show you around the villa."

Severus found Aulus at the pool and asked him to see to the Prefect while he talked to Artemisia, who he found in their bedroom napping. He woke her up.

"Sorry to wake you up, *deliciae*. But I need your advice."

"The Prefect has asked you to solve a crime, hasn't he?"

"Yes. Three crimes actually. Three murders. So far."

"Tell me about it."

And he did, recounting what had learned from the Prefect, as well as his youthful assignation with Atalanta.

"You never told me about Atalanta. Is she why you want to get involved?"

"Yes. I think I owe her something. I'm 52-years-old now. I was 16 when I spent the night with her. 36 years have passed. But yes, I still think I owe her something."

Artemisia laughed. "Well, *deliciae*. If she taught you about the arts of love, I owe her something too. I say, let's pay her back."

Severus went to the pool and motioned to the Prefect who was enjoying a swim. Paullus came out of the pool, his slave dried him off, and he put his tunic back on. Then he and Severus went back to the garden where they had conferred.

"I discussed it with my wife. I'll take the case. I want to be appointed a Special Judge, a *iudex selectus*, so that I can wield judicial powers. I want to work out of my former chambers in the Court of the Urban Prefect in the Forum of Augustus. I want all my old staff to join me. I mean my police aides Vulso and Straton from the Urban Cohort, my private secretary Alexander, my assessor Flaccus, my court clerk Quintus Proculus and my personal bodyguard, the pankratiast Crantor of Rhodes. And, of course, my wife Artemisia is an essential aide. She also loves working on my cases."

"Consider it all done. I now appoint you *iudex selectus*. I'll have the legal documents drawn up when I get back to Rome. Anything you want, just ask."

"I'll come to Rome in three days and start in."

"Will you start with the murder of Atalanta?"

"No. I will start at the beginning. With the murder of the charioteer Zephyrus of the Red faction. I'll start there."

Severus thought for a moment. "You know, Prefect, there's something peculiar about this. Why did the murderer write numbers on the cheeks of his victims? What's the point? Wouldn't it be smarter and safer not to connect one victim with another? Why did he call attention to a connection between these victims? Is it some sort of challenge?"

"A challenge. Yes. He certainly has challenged the *Vigiles*. And he certainly has challenged us in the Urban Cohort. We have no clue who the killer is or why these victims were chosen. As far as we know there's no connection between any of them."

"Evidently, then, you don't know enough. There must be a connection. A good first guess is that these three victims had one nemesis in common."

"Then find that nemesis."

"That's what I intend to do."

Later, at dinner, Severus told his family about the new *cognitio* he had agreed to take on and about the surmise that the three victims had a common nemesis who perpetrated the murders.

"Nemesis? You say, Tata," said Flavia, as she stood up from her dining couch. "I have something to show you."

She left the *triclinium* and returned carrying a Greek amphora with handles.

"I bought this in Athens when we were there five years ago. Look."

She drew everyone's attention to the orange figures painted on a black background in the classical Greek pottery style.

"It's the goddess Nemesis," she explained. "With the goddess of fortune Tyche. Nemesis is pointing at the figures of Helen of Troy and Paris carrying out their surreptitious love affair, an affair that led to the

Trojan war. Nemesis is focused on them. It's as if she's taking aim at them.

"And one more thing, one of the goddess Nemesis' symbols, besides the sword, the balance scales and the whip, is a dagger. So your case, Tata, not only fits a nemesis of the three victims committing the murders, but uses one of the goddess Nemesis' symbols to commit them. Perhaps then your murderer is not just a nemesis of the victims, but is familiar with and deliberately using the goddess Nemesis and her symbols."

"Could be," said Severus with a thoughtful look. "I'll have to keep that in mind."

III

AT THE STABLES OF
THE RED FACTION

The stables of the Red faction were located in Regio IX, near the Circus Flaminius. Close by were the stables of the Greens, Blues and Whites. These stables were much more than the place for keeping horses. They were large complexes for the entire personnel of the racing faction, consisting of at least 200-300 people for each faction. There was housing, there were training facilities, workshops, dining areas, gymnasia, and places for all the various needs of the faction and its animals.

Moreover, the needs and support for the chariots and the drivers were not simple. There were specialists for everything. For chariot racing was the greatest sport in the Empire, with millions of rabid fans, not just in Rome, but in the 100 cities across the Imperium with racetracks, where the four factions competed. Everything had to be attended to and taken care of by specialists, whether slave or free, because the fans would not tolerate anything less.

For the chariots there were carpenters for chariot construction and repairs, mesh workers for the chariot floors, and wheelwrights for the chariot wheels and axles. There were grooms for ministering to the horses and animal dieticians for feeding the horses. There were animal doctors to care for the horses and specialists to aid them by smelling the turds of the horses to check on their health. There were workers whose job it was to be on the race track during a race to throw water over their faction's horses to cool them off during the race. There were trainers and cooks and cleaners, artists and artisans, tailors, and horseshoe makers, instructors, messengers, runners, administrators and statisticians to keep meticulous and exhaustive statistics and records. There were specialists to calm the horses in the starting gates and others to tend to the starting gates. There was even a *margaritarius*, whose sole job and specialty was attaching pearls to decorate the reins of the horses. The list was almost endless.

This whole complex was headed by a *dominus factionis*, the master of the faction. He had to be a member of the Equestrian Order, like Severus. But unlike Severus who had been born into an Equestrian family, the current *dominus* of the Reds was a former charioteer, who had become wealthy by winning enough prize money -- 30,000 or 40,000 or 50,000 or 60,000 sesterces prizes -- to amass a private fortune few besides sports figures could accumulate. Some successful sports heroes made enough to meet the 400,000 sesterces qualification for the Equestrian Class, sometimes even enough to meet the million sesterces requirement for the Senatorial Order. The great Diocles had amassed a fortune of over 35 million sesterces in his career, as his monument recorded. The current *dominus* who exchanged greeting kisses with Severus had not amassed that kind of fortune, but he had made enough to become an Equestrian. When finally he had been injured and had to retire from driving, he stayed with the faction as a coach of charioteers and eventually worked his way up to *dominus*. His name was Gaius Gordianus and he greeted Judge Severus in his private dining room in the Red faction stables.

A table was set with wine and fruit and Severus and three of his assistants sat down on one side of the table, while Gordianus and two of his assistants sat down across from them. The walls of the room were painted with frescoes of chariot racing, with the predominant color of the *russata* faction naturally being russet red. This color also was predominantly displayed on mosaics and banners and upholstery throughout the stables.

Severus was accompanied by his police aides from the Urban Cohort, Caius Vulso and Publius Aelianus Straton, and his private secretary and freedman Alexander. Vulso was a centurion, a veteran of the legions, who had taken his retirement bonus and came to Rome to join the Urban Cohort. Straton as a child had been a slave of the Emperor Hadrian, but was freed at the Emperor's death and later joined the Urban Cohort. Where Vulso was rough, often brutal, though self-educated, Straton was adept at undercover work, his soulful brown eyes and ordinary appearance allowing him to blend in almost anywhere without being noticed. Alexander had once been Severus' slave, but was freed and became his private secretary and assistant. He was an intellectual with a vast knowledge of facts and information and a deep interest in liberal arts subjects that kept him and Severus in constant interesting conversation.

Gordianus had with him two assistants whom he introduced as Nicias and Paris. Nicias was a rough looking ex-chariot driver, with signs of injuries. A badly broken and clumsily repaired nose marred his face, while a skewed uneven posture, even while sitting, marred his body. Paris, on the other hand, did not look like his namesake, the lover of Helen of Troy, but more like Helen. He had gold dust in his hair and a beautiful, almost feminine face, with effeminate movements to complement the affect.

Gordianus addressed Severus. "So I'm told you have the judicial *cognitio* to find the murderer of Zephyrus."

"That's correct," replied Severus. "I'm here to gather more detailed information about his murder and I'm interested in anything you can tell me about it."

"As I've already told the Urban Prefect, I don't know much about it. Zephyrus attended a dinner party here at the Red faction. It was two days before the Kalends of May. The Floralia Games were coming to a close and the dinner was to celebrate the Red faction's part in the races and particularly those Red charioteers who had won races and prizes. It was also to honor one of our drivers who was killed in a 'shipwreck' when his chariot overturned. In any case, after dinner and during the entertainment, Zephyrus received a message tablet, read it quickly, smiled and said he had to go. Then he just got up and left. This was about the 3rd night hour. Paris here went out with him. He can tell you what happened next."

Severus looked at Paris. Paris looked at Severus, though his eyes kept darting to Vulso, who returned these looks with barely controlled laughter.

"Where did you and Zephyrus go when you left here?" asked the judge.

"I thought we were going somewhere together, but he told me to go back into the stable and go to sleep. He held up the message tablet he received, and said only that he was going to visit a friend on the Aventine Hill. Oh, I said. What friend? What's in the message?"

"He just laughed and said 'a poem'. That's what's in the message. A poem." Then he walked away.

"Did he say who the friend was?"

"He didn't tell me. But the message tablet was a fashionably small Vitellian tablet, like people use for intimate personal messages. I have to admit I felt a pang of jealousy."

"Why? What was your relationship to Zephyrus?"

"We were friends. Sometimes lovers."

"What happened to the message tablet?"

"He took it with him."

"Did he ever before mention going to visit someone on the Aventine Hill?"

"Not to me. Though he often went out on his own at night. I don't know where. He never told me."

"That's all you know?"

"That's all."

"I know some things, though," interjected Nicias.

"Tell me."

"In the middle of the night, I was awakened and asked to come with a member of the *Vigiles* to identify a body that was wearing one of our Red faction tunics. I was taken to an alley on the Aventine Hill and shown the body of a man whose throat had been cut and his head practically severed. It was Zephyrus. The number 'I' was written in blood on the left cheek of his almost severed head."

Severus addressed all three. "Did Zephyrus have any enemies you know of?"

"Everyone who roots for the Greens, Blues or Whites," countered Gordianus with a wry smile.

"Personal enemies, I mean."

"We don't know of any," replied Gordianus. "We've asked around the stables. No one mentioned any enemy. He wasn't all that popular, I have to say, because he was arrogant. But he wasn't disliked either. He was a sports hero, after all. We don't know why he was killed or who killed him. And, I expect, that's why you were given this *cognitio*, Judge Severus."

"Tell me, Gordianus, who delivered the message to Zephyrus?"

"My doorman, the *ianitor*, received it at the door from a messenger."

"Bring me the *ianitor*."

Gordianus nodded to Nicias who went out of the room and returned quickly with an old man, stooped and bent and looking tired and dull. He wore a red tunic with a red belt. And his hair was dyed a russet red. It popped into Severus' head to wonder whether the doormen at the other factions had their hair dyed green, or blue, or white.

"This is Festus," our *ianitor*.

"Festus," said Severus, "I'm a judge investigating the murder of Zephyrus. I understand he left the dinner party here when he received a message tablet and that you were the person who handed the message tablet to him. Is that right?"

"Yes."

"Who gave you the message tablet?"

"A boy. I didn't recognize him. He just appeared at the door and handed me a message tablet, saying it was for Zephyrus. Then he turned around and left."

"Describe the boy?"

"He was just a boy. Maybe 12-years-old. I didn't really notice."

"If you saw him again, would you recognize him?"

"Maybe yes, maybe no. I would have to see him. I didn't know him."

"Thank you. You may leave Festus."

When he left, Severus turned back to Gordianus. "Tell me more about Zephyrus. What was his background? How did he become a driver for the Reds?

"Zephyrus grew up in the Red faction stables. His father was a slave and a groom for the horses. Zephyrus was born a slave and joined his father as a groom when he was a child. He learned all about horses, always asking questions of charioteers about driving chariots."

Gordianus took a scroll from in front of him, unfurled it and consulting it, continued. "As a young boy

Zephyrus showed promise as a charioteer. He started racing *bigae* 2-horse chariots when he was 13. He then went on to race *trigae* 3-horse chariots and quickly advanced to racing *quadrigae* 4-horse chariots. He won his first *quadriga* victory when he was 15-years-old. He had been racing for 9 years when he died at the age of 24. During that time the scroll here says he drove in 512 races, won 53 times, came in second 142 times, and third 111 times. His prize money amounted to 1,134,324 sesterces. With those sums at his command, he bought his freedom, of course." Gordianus let the scroll roll up. "His statistics, as you can see, already rivalled the great driver Crescens of the Blue faction. Crescens died young too, but in a chariot race, not murdered in an alley in the City."

Severus addressed Gordianus, Nicias and Paris. "Do any of you know whether Zephyrus knew a courtesan named Atalanta or a shoemaker named Pedo?"

They all returned blank stares. Then Gordianus put on a supercilious smile. "You know, the drivers in our faction, the personnel of our faction, like all the other factions are celebrities, sports heroes, and are deluged with women. They follow their heroes around, many swoon at just a glance of their hero, others desire sex. There are young girls, old women, married women, upper class women, prostitutes, courtesans, you name it. Some desire to become their slaves, literally or figuratively. Charioteers are as desirable as gladiators. For the most part, we don't know their names at all. So Zephyrus might have known some courtesan or other. But who they were, we don't know. And as for shoemakers, as far as I know there must be shoemaker fans of the Circus, just like fans of almost every profession or trade, but again we wouldn't know their names."

"Do you know whether Zephyrus ever had his own high-class courtesan?"

"I know he occasionally went to high-class brothels," replied Paris, "but high-class courtesans? Not that I know of. Of course, he didn't tell me everything."

"Is there anything else you can tell me that might be relevant?"

"No. I told you everything," replied Gordianus. "It's up to you now."

Severus nodded in agreement and stood up. His assistants stood up with him and they thanked Gordianus and left.

Outside Vulso commented, "we didn't learn very much about the murder. Just the message tablet that Zephyrus received."

"That's important," replied Severus, "but you're right, there should be more. The faction is like a closed, intimate society, living together, working together. People know about each other and what's going on. There must be gossip, rumors, particularly after a murder. We should know what was being said. I find it hard to believe that they've told us everything we ought to know. I'm wary."

"I feel the same way," agreed Vulso. "So what next?"

"To the Aventine Hill. Next we're going to visit the home of Atalanta and see what we can find out about her murder."

IV

A DISCUSSION AT LUNCH

It was a nice Summer day in June. Severus and his entourage walked along the Tiber toward Regio XIII and the Aventine Hill. They passed the Theater of Marcellus and stopped into a taberna for lunch near the Temple of Hercules Victorious.

The taberna was quickly filling up with customers, but a waiter spotted Severus entering in his magistrate's toga and ushered him, Vulso, Straton and Alexander to a large table in a corner, after first moving those seated there to another table.

"*Eminentissime*," said the waiter, "our specialty is lentils. We have lentil soup, lentils with mussels, lentils with chestnuts, lentils with leeks, or we can prepare them any way you like."

"I'll start with lentil soup," said Severus, "and then I'll try the lentils with chestnuts. And some *mulsum* honey-wine to drink."

"I'll have the lentils with mussels," ordered Alexander, "and *mulsum* also."

"The same for me," said Straton.

The waiter looked to Vulso. "Do you have oysters?"

"Yes. We have an oyster specialty here, prepared with pepper, lovage, egg yolk, vinegar, *liquamen* fish sauce, oil and wine. If you wish, honey can be added as well."

"I'll have the oysters, with the added honey."

The waiter hurried off, signaled to another waiter, who brought a pitcher to the table and poured each of the men a cup of *mulsum*.

"First off," began Severus turning to Vulso, "I want you to organize a few of the Urban Cohort to go around the area and stop in at every message service office and ask if they delivered messages recently to the Red stables. I would like to find that boy the doorman mentioned, the one who delivered the message tablet for Zephyrus."

"What do think was in the message?" asked Straton.

"It was a Vitellian tablet," recalled Alexander. "So maybe a love letter. Maybe Zephyrus was going to a tryst with a woman."

"Or maybe a man, judging from Paris," added Vulso.

"Yes. It could be either," said Severus, non-committally.

"Aren't there epigrams of Martial about Vitellian tablets?" commented Alexander, "One saying, if I remember correctly, that even a girl not yet permitted to read Vitellians, knows what they desire. Another that it is not true that Vitellian tablets are only for lovers. They also are used to ask for money."

"But Zephyrus told Paris that the tablet contained a poem, didn't he?" countered Vulso. "I never heard of anyone dunning for money in poetry. I say the tablet was about love, not money."

Waiters began bringing the food to the table. Severus tasted his lentil soup and nodded in satisfaction. "Very good."

"So are my lentils with mussels," said Alexander and Straton almost simultaneously.

"I never met an oyster I didn't like," said Vulso, plunging into his dish.

Severus finished his soup and turned to his lentils with chestnuts. "Also very good," he reported.

Alexander continued discussing the case. "We're now going to the Aventine Hill. That's where the second victim, the courtesan Atalanta lived. Maybe Zephyrus was going to visit her. Maybe the intimate tablet was from her. That's just a wild guess, of course."

"We'll ask at Atalanta's house," replied Severus. "It's probably far-fetched, but you never can tell. There should be some connection between the victims. That's what the numbers I, II and III imply. Of course, the murderer could be a maniac randomly choosing his victims, but in that case, we don't know where to start. The better assumption is that the victims were connected in some way. We have to find the connection."

The judge paused for a moment and then told his aides about his one night with Atalanta, 36 years before, when he was 16, the night after receiving his toga of manhood. "That's why I decided to take on this *cognitio*," he added. "I owed her something personal, and Artemisia agreed."

"That's the upper classes for you," commented Vulso sardonically. "When they enter manhood, they get the most beautiful courtesans in the City. When I became 16, I had to masturbate."

After the laughter died down, they finished their meal and left for the Aventine Hill and the house of Atalanta.

V

AT THE HOUSE OF ATALANTA

Atalanta had lived in an *insula* apartment house half-way up the Aventine Hill. It was not an exclusive apartment house, like Severus' on the Caelian Hill, but it was not run down either. Just an ordinary 4-story *insula*.

Atalanta's apartment was on the second floor and Severus, Alexander, Vulso and Straton arrived at about the 9th day hour, as arranged by an exchange of messages. A slave doorman saw the judge in his magistrate's toga and greeted him with an excessive display of scraping in manner and words. He then bounded up the stairs to let Atalanta's mother know of the visitors' arrival. In short order, the *ianitor* came back down with a handsome middle-aged man dressed in an ordinary gray tunic. He introduced himself as Gaius Sergianus Heron.

"Novatilla, Atalanta's mother, is waiting upstairs for you. She is somewhat frail and sent me to greet you. I am in charge of the household and also Atalanta's bodyguard."

Not sure of his status, Severus did not exchange a greeting kiss, but shook hands instead. The name Heron was Greek, but Gaius Sergianus suggested he was a freedman of a Roman named Gaius Sergius. Curiously, Heron did not look at all like a bird, as his name implied. Rather, he looked noticeably well-built and strong, more like an ox than a bird.

Heron led Severus and his entourage upstairs into an apartment, where a table was set with chairs all around and fruit and wine for the guests. Already seated at the table was a rather elegant looking older woman and a very pretty younger one. Heron introduced the younger woman as Vipsania, Atalanta's daughter. The older woman introduced herself.

"I am Novatilla, Atalanta's mother. I am very glad that you have been appointed to find my daughter's killer. And after you finish with us here, Judge Severus, I wish to speak to you in private."

Severus nodded agreement. "I am at your service."

Then he looked at Novatilla, Heron and Vipsania. "I know you have already told the *Vigiles* what happened, but I want you to tell it to me."

Novatilla took a large quaff of wine. "It was a month ago, the day before the Kalends of May. We were having dinner upstairs in the apartment of a friend in this *insula*. It was after the dessert, while musical entertainment was going on. There was a very good citharist, as I remember. Anyway, while we were enjoying the music, the *ianitor* came into the *triclinium* with a message he said had just arrived for Atalanta.

He gave her a small Vitellian tablet, which she opened, read and then got up and said she had to go.

"I asked her 'what's in the message? Where are you going'? She said, looking at the tablet, 'Catullus'. Then she smiled and told Heron here and her personal slave Marilla that they didn't have to go with her. She made her excuses to the hostess and left. Later than night, the neighborhood *Vigiles* arrived at our house and told me Atalanta had been found murdered. I couldn't believe it. But it was true. It was true."

"Do any of you have any idea who murdered Atalanta?"

They all shook their heads in negative gestures. "None at all," explained Novatilla. My daughter had her own life which she mostly kept to herself. We were not that close. As mother and daughter, we often had conflicts. Anyway, as a courtesan, it was not unusual for Atalanta to receive Vitellian tablets from admirers. I just assumed this was the case when she received that message at the dinner party. And since Catullus wrote love poetry, I imagined she had received a love poem, that she knew who had sent it, and was going out to meet the sender. That's all I know."

"Do any of you know if your daughter knew a charioteer named Zephyrus of the Red faction or a shoemaker in the Subura named Pedo?"

"I never heard of either of them," replied Novatilla, "although I knew who she was a courtesan with for any length of time. However, I didn't know everyone my daughter took up with. In any case, she never lived at the Red faction and no shoemaker could afford her."

Neither Heron or Vipsania had anything to add to that.

Severus decided he wanted to hear what Atalanta's mother had to say to him in private. He therefore said to Heron and Vipsania that they were through for the moment. Atalanta's mother nodded to them, and they left the room. Vulso, Straton and Alexander left at the same time. Severus and Novatilla waited silently until they were alone. Then Severus looked inquiringly at her.

"I see Marcus, if I may call you that, you have grown into an imposing adult. I suspected as much when I first saw you on the night, around 35 years ago, wasn't it, when you assumed the *toga virilis*. Of course, I don't recognize you by looks, but by name. Your father, you see, was a special friend of mine."

Severus knew, of course, what she was referring to, though he never suspected that anyone other than he, Atalanta and his father knew about it.

"Do you know," Novatilla continued, "how your father picked my daughter for you for that night?"

"No, I don't. He never told me. And after that wonderful night, I didn't really care."

"In those days, *I* was one of the most desired courtesans in Rome. At that time, I went by the name of Briseis, which you will recognize as the name of the woman Achilles and Agamemnon fought over in the *Iliad*."

Severus nodded. "Your father asked my advice about who would be a special woman for you when you turned 16. I recommended my daughter, Atalanta, who was then 22-years-old and already an accomplished and desirable courtesan. As is common for courtesans in Greece and Rome, I raised my daughter and trained her in our profession. I taught her to play the lyre, schooled her in literature and history and culture. She first became a courtesan when she was 14 years old. She was even more beautiful than I was."

"Then I have to thank you, Novatilla, for your part in my entrance into manhood. And it is because I owe my own development in part to your daughter that I have accepted this *cognitio*."

"Good. I know I can trust you to do your utmost. But what I just told you is personal, between us. Now I have to add something that may be relevant to finding Atalanta's killer."

Severus looked at her expectantly, and with interest.

"My daughter as a high-class courtesan had many lovers during her career. She did not just command high prices, but she often provoked intense ardor and passion. And with it, extreme jealousy."

"Who?" asked Severus, realizing where she was heading.

"There was one in particular who in the past threatened to kill her if she left him. His name is Publius Pictor."

"Pictor? A painter? Or is that just an inherited *cognomen*?"

"He is in fact a painter. He has a studio in an *insula* in the Subura. He's very successful. He paints portraits and frescoes for the rich. My daughter lived with him for a number of years. She even gave up being a courtesan while she was with him. He was a passionate lover, but a jealous lover. When she left him we had to hire a bodyguard. That was Heron, who you just met. I'm sure you saw how strong Heron looked. Heron had been a wrestler at one time.

"In any event, when Atalanta moved in with Pictor, she informed her regular clients that she was retired and no longer available to them. But that did not last. Atalanta missed the money and she missed the adoration and perhaps she grew tired of Pictor. In any case, she left living with Pictor, moved back here and then took up again with clients. Pictor became a drunk and threatened to kill her if she didn't return to him. That's why we hired Heron as a bodyguard. Maybe Pictor calmed down, maybe not. But he threatened her and I believe he would be capable of murdering her."

"Thank you Novatilla. You have been most helpful. I'll look into this right away."

"I will have one of my slaves show you where in the Subura Pictor lives."

"That would be useful. And by the way, you mentioned that Atalanta had a personal slave Marilla. Is she here?"

"Marilla was my daughter's *ornatrix* and personal slave. But she was manumitted in Atalanta's will and the day after she became free, she packed all her belongings and left our house. I haven't seen or heard from her since."

As they both got up and headed to the door, Novatilla smiled at Severus. "Too bad Atalanta didn't become your courtesan."

"Thank you for the compliment. But I've been happily married for many years and have no desire for any other woman."

"Really?" said Novatilla with a coquettish smile. "That's quite unusual."

"My wife Artemisia is herself quite unusual."

"Yes. That would explain it. The goddess Fortuna must be looking out for you."

"I hope she is. I hope she is."

VI

AT THE SHOP OF A
MURDERED SHOEMAKER

The shoe store of Pedo, the murdered shoemaker, was next to the entrance to a 4-story *insula* in the Subura, the large teeming, busy, overcrowded section of the City behind the Imperial forums. Pedo lived in the back of his shop. This was a common arrangement for poor workers.

"Pedo was a recluse," said the doorman of the *insula*. "I rarely spoke to him. Or rather he rarely spoke to me. I like to speak to people. What else is there to do for a doorman? But Pedo was a recluse and surly as well. He kept to himself. I know he sometimes went out at night, but I don't know where he went or how long he stayed out. I myself am on duty here only during the day."

"I second that," added Lupus, the freedman agent for the owner of the apartment house who had been notified to be on hand when the judge arrived. Lupus had the manner of someone who is always in a rush.

He answered quickly and moved constantly, as if he was about to leave. "I collected rent from him on the first of the month, as usual, but he never talked to me. He just gave me the money and shut the door in my face. Surly is right."

"Is there anyone in the *insula* who knew him better than either of you?" asked Severus.

"Not that I know of," answered the doorman. "You would have to ask around."

Severus nodded to Straton, who understood and entered the apartment building, climbed the stairs to the second floor and began knocking on doors.

Lupus and the doorman then led Severus, Vulso and Alexander into Pedo's shop and living space. "It hasn't been re-rented yet," said Lupus, "so his belongings are still here. We're trying to find another shoemaker because the place is already set up for that. But it's the place of a murder, so a lot of people don't want to live here. We've had it ritually purified, but still no takers."

Pedo's place was one room loaded with shoes, both men's and women's. Directly in front was a table facing the door for selling the shoes, with a number of shoes displayed on it. At a 90-degree angle to the display table was a work table with partially made shoes and leather pieces waiting to be made into shoes. There was also a variety of tools on the table, awls, scissors, scrapers, among others. A chair for the shoemaker was behind the two tables with an upside-down form foot in front of it. On the walls of the shop hung other finished shoes for sale. It was close quarters inside, barely enough room for two people. Behind the store proper was a door leading to another small room — Pedo's living space. Inside was a bed, a chair, a table and a chest. It was as spare as could be, with not even a picture or a painting on the plain stucco walls.

"Where was his body found?" asked Severus.

"At the foot of the bed, right there," answered the doorman, pointing to the meager cot against one wall. "I didn't find it myself, actually. It was found one morning by a customer who entered the store to look at shoes. When she saw no one was in front she looked in the back for Pedo and saw him on the floor covered in blood. She called me as I had just arrived for work. So I went into the back and saw his body lying there. I don't know how long he had been dead, but when I saw the body and the blood, I immediately ran to the *Vigiles* station nearby and told them. Two officers came and removed Pedo's body. They said his throat had been cut and the number III written on his cheek in blood. Later one of the *Vigiles* came around and told me the body had been cremated and gave me a *signaculum* they said was around his neck."

"A *signaculum*?" said Vulso. "Like the identity pouch legionaries wear? With a piece of lead inscribed with their name so that they can be identified in case of death?"

"Yes. I put it into that chest over there. Take it if you want."

Vulso went over to the chest, opened it and began taking clothes out. "Here's the *signaculum*." He took out a small leather pouch with a leather string for hanging around the neck. He looked inside and saw the inscribed piece of lead. The name 'G. Pedo' was on it. Then Vulso continued searching the chest. "What's this?" he said, taking out a wooden instrument. "Don't you have one of these?" he said to Severus, showing him a long, thin object, with a V-shaped device on the end.

"A diopter," exclaimed Severus with surprise. "Yes, of course, I have a diopter. It's for looking at stars and planets." Severus held it to his eyes. "See, you keep a planet or a star within the v of the sighting end, so you can keep looking at it. And this is a very fine diopter."

"What's a shoemaker doing with a diopter?" asked Vulso, mystified.

"He must have been interested in astronomy," said Alexander. "What else could he have it for?"

"I agree," said Severus. "And if he had a diopter, he must have taken it out to look at the sky at night. Maybe this explains where he went at night."

"And maybe he didn't go out alone," added Alexander. "Maybe he joined some astronomy group, a *collegium* for astronomy."

"A good possibility," answered Severus. "Maybe there's a local *collegium* of astronomy buffs. We should check that out."

"There are some books in the chest too," said Vulso, handing a rolled-up scroll to Severus. The scroll had the visible signs of wear on its surface, as if it had been opened and closed many, many times. Severus opened it and began reading and smiling at the same time.

"What is it?" asked Vulso.

"It's one of my favorite books," replied Severus. "Lucian of Samosota's '*A True History*'. I've read it at least five times myself. It's about a war between inhabitants of the Moon and inhabitants of the Sun over colonizing Venus. The Moon-ites ride giant vultures while the Sun-ites oppose them with a cavalry of giant winged ants. They both have allies from the stars. So, it seems, I would have liked to talk with this shoemaker. We had interests in common." He furled up the scroll. "Let me look at the other books in the chest."

Severus walked over to the chest and started to rummage in it along with Vulso. The judge pulled out a few scrolls. "Look at this one," said the judge, reading the red label tag. "It's Aristotle's *On the Heavens*.

Severus opened the scroll at the place it was rolled up to, indicating where the reader left off.

"What was he reading?" asked Vulso.

"He left the scroll furled to where Aristotle discusses observational proof that the Earth is spherical. You know, it's round shape can be seen in an eclipse of the Moon where the Earth comes between the Sun and the Moon. Also, the fact that the stars and constellations set and rise as one travels north or south proves the path traveled is over a curved surface, and not a flat one. Over a flat surface, there would be no movement of the stars and constellations. There is also Aristotle's theoretical proof based on the idea that the Earth is at the center of the Universe. If it is, then the Earth must have been created by matter falling toward the center, just like when we drop something it always falls down. The only shape the Earth could take from matter falling down from all directions is spherical."

Severus picked up a few other scrolls and looked at the label tags. "Hmm. Eratosthenes, Poseidonius, all on astronomy. I think I'll take these scrolls and the diopter for myself and my son Quintus, who loves astronomy books. Pedo no longer has any use for them."

Vulso pulled out another item. "This will interest you even more," he said as he handed Severus a small Vitellian tablet. Severus opened it and read it out loud. "…Give me a thousand kisses, then a hundred, then another thousand, then a second hundred, and then another thousand, then a hundred…"

"Catullus, isn't it?" said Alexander.

"Yes. From his poem, addressed to his lover Lesbia. 'Let us live, Lesbia, and let us love,' it begins. The lines written here are an excerpt."

"So," concluded Straton, "this must be the same sort of Vitellian tablet that both Zephyrus the charioteer and Atalanta received. Pedo got one too."

"Probably," added Severus, "But there's another possibility."

"What could that be?" replied Alexander.

Severus returned a wry smile and put the tablet in a fold of his toga. "Maybe he wrote it."

Later that night, in bed with Artemisia, Severus told her about what they found at Pedo's. She was interested, but had something else on her mind. Severus noticed it.

"What's on your mind?"

"It's about Flavia," said Artemisia. "Aulus thinks he has a friend who Flavia might really like. He wants to introduce them."

"Who is he?"

"He's an army buddy of Aulus. His name is Publius Flamma. Aulus says he's handsome, has a good sense of humor and is a serious person. He's also from an Equestrian family, like us."

"Will Flavia go for a soldier? I don't think that's her type."

"Aulus says Flamma is only in the army because his family made him join up. It's a family tradition. Flamma really wants to get out of the army and since his father died recently during the plague, he feels free to leave the army as soon as he can. His real interests, Aulus says, are poetry and playing the cithara."

"Poetry and the cithara. Those are the two things Flavia most loves. Aulus may be right. It sounds like this Flamma might really appeal to her. How does Aulus want to work the introduction?"

"He's already told Flavia about Flamma and she's interested. Aulus has set up a meeting in the nearby park for tomorrow afternoon. Both are to bring their citharas and play together and get to know each other."

"Will Aulus stay with them?"

"Of course. And I'll be there too, but we will not hover. We'll let them get acquainted. That's the idea, after all."

"I hope this works out. Let me know what happens."

"Of course, *deliciae*."

Severus smiled warmly at Artemisia. Artemisia smiled warmly at him. They snuggled up to each other and their warmth turned quickly into heat and then into passion. It was quite a while before they got any sleep.

SCROLL II

VII

AT PICTOR'S ART STUDIO

Well before the 10th hour, Severus, Vulso and Alexander walked up the back staircase of the Forum of Augustus and entered the Subura, Rome's most lively, busy, noisy, dense, boisterous inhabited area. The Subura was packed with apartment buildings, markets, shops, and people of every kind going about their lives. One of Novatilla's slaves led the way to the *insula* of Publius Pictor, the artist who the mother of Atalanta had accused of threatening her daughter's life.

Severus was dressed in his official magistrate's white toga, with its reddish-purple hem. It helped clear a path through the bustling street crowds in the Subura, people naturally steering clear of a Roman judge. Vulso wore a red military tunic with a wide military belt, another person pedestrians preferred to avoid. Alexander and their guide both wore elegant Greek style tunics. As a result, as many people on the street bumped into them as walked around them.

Messages exchanged with Pictor the day before had set up the meeting for the 5th hour of the morning and Severus and his party ambled casually through the crowded streets. They stopped once at the sidewalk counter of a *thermopolium* hot shop for a snack, when the luscious aroma of Lucanian sausages tempted Severus to have one. The others just stood by, except for Alexander who checked the time with his pocket sun dial and then announced, "It's getting close to the 5th hour, judge. We'd better move along."

Severus downed his sausage and the group walked briskly the rest of the way, occasionally having to elbow through idlers clogging the streets, and occasionally slowing to watch a street side barber shaving a customer or a doctor treating a patient.

When they reached Pictor's *insula,* they were met at the entrance by a young boy who was there waiting for them. He wore a plain gray tunic, stained with paint splotches. He introduced himself as Glaukon, a slave of the painter Pictor. Immediately he began bowing obsequiously and apologizing because his master was not there to meet the judge. He had gone to a store nearby to buy supplies.

"He will be right back," assured Glaukon. "I'm sure he will. He is expecting you."

"He should be here when a Roman judge is expected," replied Severus, a bit testily, though in fact he didn't care one way or another. He dismissed the slave who had brought them to the *insula* with thanks and then followed Glaukon up the stairs to the second floor, where Pictor had his studio and living space.

Immediately upon entering, a strong but not unpleasant smell of solvents and paints greeted them. The studio was a large room with wide open shutters to let the light through the windows. It was crammed with paintings, paints, brushes and easels along with a supply of wood panels and linen and parchment canvases to paint on. There was hardly any place without a painting or painting paraphernalia. At first glance, many of the paintings seemed finished, but others were obviously unfinished. Some were just drawings, others partially painted. Some paintings were of mythological scenes, some nature scenes with trees and water, some scenes of everyday life, some portraits of people. The colors were sometimes subtle, sometimes vibrant.

There was one large table with a marble slab for grinding pigments and combining the powder with a solvent to make paint.

"I see you grind your own paints," said the judge

Glaukon eagerly began an explanation, his voice full of pride. "Yes. That's my job. Look at all my colors." He pointed to bowls of red, white, black, yellow, blue and green pigments and powder already ground from a hard source of colored material. He held up a flat-bottomed grinder. "With this I mix the colored powder on the marble slabs to make paints, and then mix the colors with egg for tempura or wax for encaustics.

"I have two kinds of red, a red ochre from Sinope on the Euxine Sea, the other cinnabar, the best of which comes from silver mines outside of Ephesus. You may recognize the bright scarlet of cinnabar as the color painted on the faces of statues of Jupiter as well as on the faces of victorious generals celebrating triumphs. I also have two blues, one ground azurite from Armenia, another from Cyprus. My white comes from the island of Melos. The green is ground malachite. My yellow is yellow ochre from Attica in Greece. I could go on and on because making paint is what I love to do, but perhaps you want to look at the paintings rather than the paints."

"Both are interesting," said Severus, "so we'll just look around." He was enjoying the combined rush of smells, colors and paintings. In fact, the whole display of art and its production delighted both his nose and his eyes. Alexander and Vulso also strolled about the studio looking at the art. Severus was focused on one painting sitting on an easel by an open window, when the door burst open and a thin, middle aged man dressed in a paint-stained tunic came in.

"I am Publius Pictor, an artist of great talent but little money." He looked at Severus in his magistrate's toga. " 'What an artist is dying in me' were the Emperor Nero's last words. What an artist is alive in me, are my living words." Pictor had no bags of supplies with him, and he seemed more than a little drunk, slurring his words.

"I am at your service, *eminentissime*" Pictor said in an exaggerated way, with a kind of mockery in his voice. "Perhaps you would like to buy a painting? Or commission one? Or just browse. Yes, first browse and then decide." He lurched into a chair and took a deep breath.

Severus turned to Vulso. "Sober him up."

Vulso smiled and turned to Glaukon. "Give me a large cup of water."

Glaukon dipped a large metal cup into a bucket and handed it to Vulso, who then grabbed Pictor by the hair, held his face up and threw water into it."

"By Hercules! Why did you do that, you monster?" He wiped his face with his arm.

"To sober you up, you drunk. Do you want another dose?"

"No, no. I'm sober. I'm sober." He turned to the judge. His manner became respectful. "*Eminentissime*, didn't your message say you wanted to talk to me about Atalanta? You said I could help you find her murderer."

"Yes."

"What do you want to know. I want to help all I can. She was the love of my life."

"Tell me about you and her. She lived with you, didn't she?"

"Yes. For about a year. A wonderful year. A glorious year."

"She was a courtesan. A very expensive courtesan. How is it that she lived with you?"

"Ah. A story to be engraved in stone, to be written in iambic verse, to be preserved for the ages."

"Just tell me what happened."

"I need a drink. Some wine, Glaukon."

"First the story," said Severus. "Then the wine."

"Then I will tell you quickly. But first you have to know the story of the greatest painter of all, Apelles, and of Alexander the Great and his favorite concubine Pancaspe."

"What does that have to do with what I am asking?"

"What does it have to do with it? Everything. The elder Pliny writes about it, in his Natural History volume about painting and painters. Yes, it is history repeating itself. That's what it is. You see, Alexander the Great had a much beloved concubine Pancaspe, whose beauty he admired so much that he wanted the great Apelles to paint her in the nude. Well, while painting Pancaspe, Apelles fell in love with her. And so Alexander, out of admiration for the artist, gave her to Apelles. That was about 500 years ago. But two years ago, a Roman General had a courtesan, Atalanta, who he wanted to have painted in the nude. I was selected to paint her. And what happened? Just as Apelles fell in love with Pancaspe, I fell in love with Atalanta. And she with me. So she left the General, who was paying her quite well to be his courtesan, and moved in with me. That's how we met and that's how we became lovers."

"Who was the General?"

"Someone retired and repulsive, with one arm and one eye but lots of money."

"His name?"

"Lucius Manilius Crispinus. He lives on the Caelian Hill."

"So you and Atalanta became lovers. But what happened then? Was Heron her bodyguard at that time?"

"Heron. That big idiot. No. What happened was her mother, Novatilla. That's what happened."

"Tell me about it?"

"Novatilla hated me. But even more than that, she needed Atalanta, who was her main source of income. Atalanta, when she moved in with me, gave up being a courtesan. I wasn't paying her anything to live with me. I couldn't afford her anyway. I'm not one of those painters like Parrhasius whose painting of the high priest of Cybele was sold to the Emperor Tiberius for 6 million sesterces, nor even like Cydias whose painting of the argonauts sold for 144,000 sesterces. I make a living, but barely. Still, she gave up being a courtesan and became my lover and I hers. Oh, if you only knew how glorious that was. But how could you? You did not know her." Severus smiled inwardly to himself, while Pictor smiled outwardly. Both had memories of Atalanta. "Her mother forced her back to working as a courtesan. And not just her mother. The whole family pressured her. Her children also. They all needed the money she earned."

"Her children? I know she had a daughter, Vipsania. I met her at Atalanta's house. Were there more?"

"She was a courtesan and contraception does not always work. During the course of her working, she conceived at least twice, so she told me. Other than Vipsania I don't know who the other child or children are, or even if they're alive. I know that one died of an infection shortly after birth. Ask Novatilla. She probably knows."

"I will. But tell me, I heard something disturbing about you. I heard that when Atalanta left you, you threatened to kill her?"

"Who told you that? Oh, you don't have to tell me. It was her mother. Yes, I threatened to kill her if she left me. But it was out of despair, out of anger. I could never do anything like that. I loved her. If you want to know who could have killed her, talk to that General, to Crispinus. She was afraid of him, of what he would do when she left him. My threat was an idle one, but maybe his anger wasn't."

"Is there anything else you can tell me about her?"

"It's all personal. It's all within me. But if you want to find out more about her, look at her paintings."

"What do you mean, her paintings?"

"While she was living with me, she took up painting. She happened to read Pliny's book on painters and came across the section on famous women artists. Timarete, the daughter of Micon. Irene, the daughter of Cratinus. Iaia of Cyzicus, who painted a portrait of herself using a metal mirror and whose portrait painting commanded higher prices than the most celebrated portrait painters of her day. Iaia painted in Rome and in Neapolis. When Atalanta read that, she said she always wanted to be a painter as a child and she then asked me to give her lessons and I did. As it turned out, she was a very good student, a very good artist. Here, I'll show you some of her works."

Pictor got up and walked to a far corner of the room where there were painted wooden panels stacked up, one in front of another. "These are hers."

Severus started to look through them. There were five painted panels.

"They're all portraits."

"Yes. She liked doing portraits. There's one of me, as you can see."

"Oh yes. It's quite recognizable." Severus sifted through the others, and pulled one out.

"Who is this?"

"Oh. The charioteer and his trace horse. Yes, he was a very good driver for the Reds. I heard he recently died in a crash in the Circus. You can see his name painted on the panel, Zephyrus, and the name of his horse as well, Compressor."

Severus, Vulso and Alexander looked at each other in astonishment. Zephyrus they all knew was the first murder victim, the one before Atalanta.

"How did she happen to paint him?"

"I don't know. I know he came here once or twice to pose. I used to talk to him about chariot racing. He gave me tips for betting. One time she went to the Red faction stables to paint his horse."

"Who are these other people?"

"Just ordinary people who she wanted to paint. That one there, the third panel is of a shoemaker. You can see he's working on a sandal in the painting. You can also see a whole workshop with shoes displayed in the painting. I think she bought her shoes from him. I don't know his name or where the shoe shop is."

Once again Severus, Vulso and Alexander looked at each other in astonishment, as the same thought flashed through each of their minds. Could the shoemaker in the painting be Pedo, the third murder victim?

"Did the shoemaker ever come here for a portrait?"

"Not that I know of. She probably painted him at his workshop. You can see it in the painting. The next one is a man I know nothing about." It was a painting of a middle-aged man, with a weak face, high cheek-bones and unfocused dark eyes. He wore a green tunic with a blue belt and was seated on an armchair reading a scroll.

"The painting behind that, however, is a painting of Maro and Marilla."

"Marilla? Wasn't she the personal slave of Atalanta?"

"Yes. Marilla is Atalanta's slave, or was until Atalanta died. Then Marilla was freed by her will. Maro is a freedman of mine who worked here mixing paints, preparing painting surfaces, *et cetera*. The day Marilla was freed she ran off with Maro. I haven't seen either of them since. I don't know where they are."

"You say Maro worked here. Did Marilla serve Atalanta while she was living here? Is that how Marilla and Maro met?"

"I believe so."

"Were they lovers?"

"They ran away together, so they must have been."

"Where does Maro live?"

"I know he lives in an *insula* in the Subura, not far from here. At least that's what he said. But I've never been to his apartment and I don't know where it is."

"I'll have to take these paintings with me, all except the one of you. You'll get them back at a later time."

Pictor shrugged. "Whatever you wish, *eminentissime*."

Vulso gathered up the paintings and asked Glaukon for some wrapping paper, which he produced along with string, for Vulso to pack the paintings.

"By the way, Pictor. Do you happen to have a painting of Atalanta?"

"I do. More than one. I loved painting her, in the nude and clothed."

"Show me the best likeness of her."

Pictor went to another corner of the room and pulled out a rolled-up parchment. He unfurled it and showed it to Severus. He didn't recognize her at all. But, of course, he had seen Atalanta only once, many years before and it was dimly lit in the room and she was 35 years younger. But judging by Pictor's painting of her, Atalanta was still a beautiful woman. In this painting, she was clothed in a clinging tunic.

"I'll take this painting of her with me as well," said the judge, handing it to Vulso.

"Thank you, Pictor. Now you can have your wine."

"Now I don't need it. Now, what I really want to do is cry."

VIII

PLANS ARE MADE

The next morning a meeting was held in Judge Severus' chambers in the Forum of Augustus. All his aides were there: Urban Cohort members Vulso and Straton, private secretary Alexander, bodyguard and pankratiast Crantor, court clerk Quintus Proculus, and wife and confidante Artemisia. Even his former assessor Gaius Sempronius Flaccus took time off from his busy legal practice to attend. Wine and fruit were placed on the table they sat around.

"Before we make our plans, Straton has something to report."

Straton held up the wood painting of a shoemaker working on a sandal. "I took this to the *insula* of Pedo yesterday afternoon and showed it around to the doorman and various occupants of the apartment building. There's no doubt. This is a painting of Pedo, the third murder victim. However, no one had any information about who painted it or when. Also no one was able to identify the painting of Atalanta, which I also showed around."

"It's sufficiently interesting, though," said Severus, "that Atalanta, the second murder victim painted portraits of the first and third murder victims and that all three are connected in some way to the studio of Pictor. What do we make of this?" He looked around. "Anyone have any ideas?"

Vulso answered first. "Yes. Maybe Pictor murdered them all. His claim to love Atalanta is just pretense. He killed her for leaving him, just as he threatened."

"What about the others?" rejoined Severus.

"I don't know yet," answered Vulso. "But as of now, my bet is on Pictor having killed all three."

Artemisia broke in. "Maybe so, Vulso. But maybe not. One thing I want to know now is who is the unidentified man in the other portrait? If two people whose portraits Atalanta painted have already been murdered, along with herself, maybe that man will be the next victim."

"Or maybe he's the killer," suggested Flaccus.

"But what about Maro and Marilla, Atalanta's former slave," said Proculus. "I think we must find her. It's likely she accompanied Atalanta when she went out to paint. Maybe she knows something about Pedo, or about the unidentified man her mistress painted."

"More than that," replied Artemisia. "And this is just speculation, but maybe Maro and Marilla killed Atalanta so that Marilla would be set free and be free to run away with her lover."

"We certainly can't exclude that possibility," replied Severus

"He turned to Vulso and Straton. "How do we find Marilla?"

Straton answered. "Since Marilla was Atalanta's slave, we should go back to Atalanta's house and talk again with her family. Maybe one of them knows things about Marilla that would help us find her. As for Maro, Pictor told us he lives in the Subura. Where? He didn't know. There are thousands of apartment buildings in the Subura, so we can't check them all, but we can start by asking the local *Vigiles*, who know the neighborhoods they're in. Maybe someone will recognize Maro or Marilla."

"Asking the *Vigiles* will probably take a lot of time," replied the judge, "so I'll start by going back to Atalanta's house tomorrow and questioning all the members of the household. Maybe one of them knows where Marilla is.

"And by the way, I'm having all these portraits copied by an artist and his aides who often work making drawings for the police and courts. We'll have three copies of each of them to show around by this afternoon, I'm told. We should show everyone the picture of the unidentified man reading a scroll. Maybe someone will know who he is. He could be a possible victim or a possible murderer, as has been suggested. But as of now, he may be neither. We should keep our minds open to all possibilities."

He turned to Straton. "By the way, have you made any progress in locating the boy who delivered the message with the love poem to Atalanta? It was the poem that called her away from the dinner party to her death."

"No. I've checked with the messenger services in the area, but no luck. Whoever sent the tablet with the poem may have randomly picked a boy in the streets and paid him to deliver the message. But I'm having two members of the Urban Cohort ask around with boys in the streets. Maybe we'll find something eventually, but there's nothing yet. The *Vigiles* say we'll never find the boy because people who pick boys off the street to deliver messages also pay them extra to keep quiet. So it's likely, even if we find the right boy, he will deny it."

Alexander added a thought. "Maybe we should take a picture of Atalanta to the Red faction stables and show it around. If she painted Zephyrus' horse there, possibly someone will remember her and give us some more information about her connection to Zephyrus the charioteer."

"Good idea. Who wants to do that?"

"I'll go," spoke up Crantor, Severus' bodyguard. "I like horses."

"And I'll go with him," added Straton.

"Good. Pick up a copy of Atalanta's portrait later today and take it to the Red faction stables. Also take with you pictures of Maro and Marilla and the unknown man painted by Atalanta. Show them around too." Severus thought for a moment. "I will revisit Atalanta's household and talk to her mother and daughter and bodyguard again. They're not in the clear, as far as I'm concerned. In any event, they can give me information about Marilla. Also. I want to show them the painting of the unknown man with a scroll. Maybe they can identify him."

"I have another issue to bring up," interjected Artemisia. Everyone looked at her. "I want to know why the killer wrote the numbers one, two and three on the faces of his victims. What is the point?"

"The killer wanted to connect them?" answered Flaccus.

"Yes. But why?" shot back Artemisia. "Wouldn't it be harder to find the killer if he hadn't numbered his victims? There would be no connection at all between them. Why is the killer announcing his crimes? What for? Why is he making himself easier to find, rather than more difficult?"

"Those are good questions," answered Severus. "I've been troubled by that aspect of the case myself. As you say, *deliciae,* why is the killer making it easier to find him by connecting his victims, rather than more difficult, by not connecting them? The answer, I suppose, will have to await further developments.

"Right now, I have an appointment in an hour to visit the General Crispinus, the man Atalanta left to become the lover of Pictor. A man, who we are told threatened Atalanta's life because she left him. Vulso and Straton, I want you both to come with me. Probably the General will feel more comfortable in the presence of soldiers, even if he might be uncomfortable being questioned by a Roman judge."

Vulso laughed. "I happen to know Crispinus personally, judge. We once served together with the legion I Minervia in Germania. And I can assure you that it's for us to be comfortable with the General. Not him with us."

IX

GENERAL CRISPINUS

Later that afternoon, Severus, Straton and Vulso were met at the entrance to General Crispinus' *domus* on the Caelian Hill by two slaves, one wearing a placard with the number VIII around his neck, the other with number XII. This practice of numbering slaves rather than naming them, though insulting and depersonalizing, was not uncommon. Severus, however, disliked it and immediately disliked the General for doing it.

They were escorted through the vestibule into the atrium, where the General was awaiting their arrival. He was dressed in a red military tunic, with a wide military belt, the same as Vulso wore. Severus had on his red-purple bordered magistrate's toga.

General Crispinus was a forbidding looking person. His face was deeply furrowed with lines and wrinkles, his glance almost menacing. His one good eye bored into whoever he was looking at. His other eye was covered by a black patch. Grim and haughty, he inspired immediate fear and dislike. At least that's the way the General appeared to Severus and Alexander as he glared at them when they entered the atrium. But when the General saw Vulso, his whole manner changed. Startled, he smiled broadly and said, "Caius Vulso? Is that really you?"

Vulso saluted him, right hand to forehead, palm down, and smiled back. "Yes, Lucius. It's me." They embraced each other and exchanged a kiss on the lips, Roman style between equals.

"It's been a long time." The General actually smiled and then turned to Severus. "Vulso and I served together with the legion I Minervia at Bonn in *Germania Inferior* when we were young. Before I was a General, before he was a Centurion. Those were the days, weren't they, Caius." He made a fist. "We gave it to those Chatti barbarians, didn't we."

"We certainly did, Lucius."

"What do they say about the Roman army?" They chanted in unison. "Our drills are like bloodless battles. Our battles are like bloody drills."

"After your judge finishes here, Caius, I hope you stay and we can reminisce."

"I would like that very much."

"So would I. I'll have lunch brought in. Are oysters still your favorite dish?"

"Of course."

The General turned to the slave stationed at the entrance to the atrium. "Eight, tell Three to go to the market and get a lot of oysters for lunch and tell Five to make lunch for me and my guest, with the oysters the main course. And bring out a bottle of my best Falernian wine to go with them."

"Yes, *domine*," said slave number VIII as he hurried off to carry out his assignment.

The General turned to the judge. "Come into the *tablinum*, where we can sit down and you can ask your questions." He led them into the room behind the atrium where there was a table already set out with cups of wine and a bowl of fruit and motioned everyone into chairs around the table.

"We're here, General, to talk about your former courtesan Atalanta."

"Yes. Your message said she had been murdered. That's too bad. She was a very special courtesan and I paid her well to live with me. She was well educated and could even discuss military history with me. And she was a wonderful musician on the lyre, both playing and singing along. How was she killed?"

"Her throat was cut from behind. She was found in an alley."

"What was she doing there?"

"We don't know. She was at a dinner with friends, when a message came for her and she got up and left. The message was a love poem by Catullus. We don't know who sent the message or where she went."

"So why do you come to me? I had nothing to do with her murder. I liked her." He almost sneered at the suggestion.

"We have been told that you threatened to kill her when she left you for a painter. Is that true?"

"*Nugax*. Nonsense. One courtesan is more or less like another and when Atalanta left, I simply hired another. I had no reason to kill her and I would never do such a thing. What for?"

"Did you hire the painter Pictor to paint her in the nude?"

"Yes."

"How did you choose Pictor to paint her?"

"He was the only painter I knew. He painted the wall fresco in my bedroom. So I gave him the commission to paint Atalanta."

"How did Pictor come to paint the bedroom fresco?"

"One of my slaves found him." He went to the entrance to the *tablinum* and called out to the slaves.

Eight came in and the General asked him how they had found Pictor to paint his bedroom wall.

"I don't know. Someone recommended him. I'll ask around."

The General shrugged. "I don't bother myself with such trivialities. Next question."

Severus nodded to Straton, who took out a copy of the painting of the man with the scroll painted by Atalanta.

"Do you recognize him at all?"

Crispinus looked at the parchment. "No."

"Can you show it around to your household?"

"Eight, take this painting around to everyone in the household and ask if anyone knows him."

Eight took the parchment from Straton and left the room. "That will take a while, but I'll have an answer for Vulso by the time we finish lunch. So, unless there's anything else, judge, you can go."

"A final question, General. Did you happen to know a chariot driver for the Reds named Zephyrus or a shoemaker named Pedo?"

"I know, or knew Zephyrus. I heard that he died. I don't know any shoemakers."

"How did you know Zephyrus?"

"At one time I was very interested in chariot racing, taking my cue from our departed co-Emperor Lucius Verus. If you'll remember he was a great fan of the Greens and used to hang around the Green stables, regularly having dinner there, hobnobbing with the drivers, even bringing delicacies to feed to his favorite horse, Volucer. I did not go that far, but I did occasionally have dinner at the Red stables, since the Reds are my favorite faction. I met Zephyrus there and occasionally spoke with him, but I can't say I really knew him."

"Thank you, General." Severus and Straton then got up and headed out of the *domus*.

Vulso stayed for an excellent lunch of oysters and hours of reminiscences with his old army buddy. He left later that afternoon with the painting in hand and reported to the judge that no one recognized the man with the scroll.

"Do you think he had anything to do with Atalanta's murder?" asked the judge.

"Crispinus? No. Not at all. He only murders people following orders and that's not murder, that's patriotism."

X

STRATON AND CRANTOR RETURN TO THE RED FACTION STABLES

The next morning at the 3rd hour Straton and Crantor showed up at the Red faction stables and asked to speak with Nicias, the chief assistant to Gordianus, the *dominus* of the Reds. Nicias came out to the vestibule to meet them.

"What do you want now?" he asked gruffly, annoyance in his voice.

"When we were here last," replied Straton, "we asked whether anyone knew a courtesan named Atalanta, whether Zephyrus might have known her."

"So?"

"No one knew. But now we have found a connection between them. Atalanta, besides being a courtesan, had become a painter and we have a painting of Zephyrus and his horse Compressor painted by her. She painted Zephyrus at an art studio in the Subura, but she must have come here to the stables to paint the

75

horse. We want to talk to someone in the stables, perhaps a groom, who might remember her being here and painting the horse."

"Come with me. I'll take you to the stable where Compressor is kept and you can talk to the groom or anyone else you want there."

"That's what we want. Thank you."

Nicias led them through the building and out back to the actual stables where the horses were. In addition to the visible damage to his face and posture, Nicias walked with a serious limp. He led them slowly down a row of stalls until he stopped in front of one and pointed at the horse standing in the stall.

"That's Compressor." He then called out for a groom.

A middle-aged man with a hang-dog look appeared. Nicias introduced him to Straton and Crantor as the slave Phlius, and then limped away.

"Phlius," said Straton, "are you the groom who takes care of Compressor?:

"Yes, I am. Compressor and several other horses as well."

"How long have you been seeing to Compressor?"

"Since he was born, three years ago."

"Just to make certain, Compressor was the trace horse of Zephyrus' chariots. Is that correct?"

"Yes. This horse is one of the main reasons Zephyrus won so many races. Compressor not only understands his role in a race, but he and Zephyrus had a special understanding. They raced very well together."

"Do you remember a time when an artist came to paint Compressor?"

"Oh yes. That woman. I don't remember her name. But Zephyrus brought her here and asked me to help her in any way she asked. She was an older woman, but very beautiful. As was her younger slave girl, whose name I was never told. She carried in the easel and paint box and wood boards for the painter."

"How long did she take to paint Compressor?"

"A few hours."

"And then she left?"

"Not exactly."

"What do you mean, not exactly."

"After she finished and was packing up, I went to tell Zephyrus she had finished. Zephyrus had told me earlier to tell him when she was done."

"Then what?"

"Then Zephyrus told the slave girl to take the painting equipment and leave and asked the painter to come with him. That's all I saw." He stopped, thought a moment, and added almost slyly, "But, of course, I heard things."

"What did you hear?"

Phlius began mulling over something.

"Both Zephyrus and the courtesan, her name was Atalanta, have been murdered. You should tell us whatever you know, or heard, because it may help us find out who killed Zephyrus."

"Then I'll tell you. The gossip was that Zephyrus got this Atalanta to go to his room and raped her. He bragged about it afterwards."

"To you?"

"No, not to me. But to other charioteers probably, and to Nicias, I'm sure. Everyone heard about it. It was all over our stables."

"Thank you, Phlius. We'll talk to Nicias."

Straton and Crantor then went back into the main building and asked for Nicias, who soon reappeared, looking even more annoyed. "Now what?"

"The woman who painted Compressor was a courtesan named Atalanta. She, like Zephyrus, was murdered. We want to know what happened between them."

Nicias thought a bit. "I don't betray confidences, but in this case they're both dead, so it doesn't matter what they did. And anyway, Zephyrus bragged to everyone what happened."

Straton and Crantor looked at him expectantly.

"I'll just tell you what Zephyrus told me and everyone else. He said he was smitten by this woman, but she refused to sleep with him. He said he got her to come to our stables to paint his horse and then contrived to get her into his room. He made advances but she again refused him. So he raped her. He said he never raped anyone because, well, as a famous charioteer he could have most anyone he wanted. But her refusal only stimulated him further. He then used force to have her. Afterwards, he bragged that he really enjoyed raping her and recommended rape to everyone he told the story to. We all laughed at him, thinking he wasn't serious. But he was."

Straton and Crantor left and immediately returned to the Forum of Augustus to tell Judge Severus what they had learned.

"So Zephyrus raped Atalanta," said Severus. "That would give her a good reason to kill him. But then who killed her?"

They all hunched their shoulders and spread their hands out wide. "We just don't know," said Straton.

"Yet," added Severus. "We just don't know yet. And also, it just occurred to me, there's another reason why it may be important to find Marilla. This is because she accompanied Atalanta to the Red faction stables to paint the horse, carrying her painting equipment. So maybe she did the same thing when Atalanta went to paint Pedo, the shoemaker at his shoe shop. Maybe Marilla knows something about the relationship of Atalanta and Pedo. In other words, we now must find Marilla."

XI

SEVERUS RETURNS TO ATALANTA'S HOME

The next morning at the 10th hour, Severus, Artemisia, Vulso and Alexander showed up at Atalanta's *insula* on the Aventine Hill, as had been arranged by messages exchanged the previous day. And as had been requested by the judge, every member of the household was present: Atalanta's mother Novatilla, Atalanta's daughter Vipsania, and Atalanta's bodyguard Heron

They all sat around a table as Severus began. "The first thing I would like to know is, where is Marilla? I have to talk to her. Does anyone here know?"

Vipsania raised her hand. "I had lunch with her yesterday."

"Where did you find her?"

"We had lunch in a taberna in the Subura. She sent me a message the day before wanting to meet me for lunch. We're about the same age, you see, and we were friends, even while she was my mother's slave.

Now she's free and we're on equal terms, so we're both happy about that. And after lunch we went to her apartment to just talk and talk some more."

"Where is her apartment?"

"I don't know the address. Somewhere off the Clivus Suburanus. I can take you there."

"Vulso. Go with her now and bring Marilla to my chambers as soon as you can. Vipsania, will you show him the way?"

Vipsania got up and she and Vulso exchanged interested, almost lascivious, looks. "I'd be glad to show him the way."

Severus addressed Novatilla. "Novatilla, I would like to have my wife go into Atalanta's room and just look around. Maybe there are some letters there, or writings, or some things that can shed light on what happened to her. Is that all right with you?"

"Of course. I'll take Artemisia to her room." Both she and Artemisia got up and walked down a corridor to Atalanta's room.

Severus then addressed Atalanta's bodyguard, Heron. "Heron, when did you become the bodyguard for Atalanta? Were there specific threats? Was there anyone in particular she was afraid of?"

"I was hired as her bodyguard about a year ago. I was told she had been raped and didn't want anything like that to happen again. I was to accompany her from then on whenever she wanted."

"Did she tell you who raped her?"

"No. She never did. But I know she thought about it. It made her angry. Every now and then it just sort of popped into her mind and she became livid, paced around the room, muttering to herself, her face contorted in anger and her fists clenched. I wish I could have gotten my hands on whoever raped her, but she never said who it was."

A short while later, Artemisia came back carrying a large basket. "It's filled with papers," she reported to her husband. "Letters, scribblings, a book that looks to be a diary of sorts. I'll have to look these over."

"We'll take these then," said Severus to Novatilla. "They'll be returned shortly."

"You're welcome to look through them. I hope they shed some light on who killed my daughter."

"Maybe they will. If we find anything, we'll let you know. But now I have to ask you a question that may be painful, but we have to follow every lead."

Novatilla looked at him with some anxiety showing on her face.

"We heard that Atalanta was once raped. Did she tell you about it?"

"She told me she was raped. That's true. But she never told me who did it. That's one reason why I had to get away from that drunken painter, Pictor. And it's why we hired Heron as her bodyguard. From then on, he was to go with her whenever she thought there might be some danger to her."

"Why do you suppose she didn't tell you who raped her?"

"I don't know. We didn't always have the best of relationships. Often she didn't tell me about her life, except to say it was none of my business. But I know the rape occurred when she was living with that creepy artist Pictor, although he wasn't the one who raped her. She had become a painter herself and I gather that it was someone she painted who raped her. But that's only a guess. She never told me. I know it ate at her. She became angry whenever she thought about it. But something prevented her from saying who it was or from doing anything about it. Do you know who it was who raped her?"

"Yes. I do. It was victim number one, the chariot driver Zephyrus."

"Oh? That's a surprise. The rapist and his victim both murdered? Well, had she not been victim number two, she would have been glad someone murdered her rapist."

Heron seconded the thought. "If I had known, I would have killed him myself. Probably that's why she never told me. He was too famous. A sports hero. But you say he was murder victim one. I thought he died in the Circus, a crash during a race."

"That's the story the Red faction put out. Otherwise, if it were known he had been murdered, Red fans would have blamed the Blues or the Greens or the Whites and might seek revenge against one of their drivers."

"So that's why she didn't tell me," concluded Heron. "If I had killed Zephyrus, some Red fan would have killed me in revenge."

"Yes. That's possible," replied Severus, though he doubted that was the reason for Atalanta's silence about the matter. But it remained curious why both the rapist and the woman he raped were murdered as victim one and victim two. Did the killer know about the rape? Did that play a part in the two murders, or was there some other reason. Another conundrum, thought Severus to himself.

XII

MARILLA

Vipsania led Vulso to the *insula* in the Subura where Marilla lived with Maro. Marilla was home when they arrived, dressed in an ordinary gray tunic with a gray headscarf, cleaning the apartment. She looked to be in her mid-thirties. She wasn't beautiful in the soft way of many upper-class Roman women, but she was handsome in the way of many lower-class Roman women, their lined faces testifying to their harder lives, but displaying experience and worldliness. Marilla was happy to see her friend Vipsania, but somewhat wary of Vulso, who she didn't know and who looked official, dressed in his red tunic and wide military belt. Vipsania calmed her.

"He's with the Urban Cohort. He's working for the Special Judge who is going to find my mother's murderer. I know you want to help."

"What can I do? I know nothing about it."

"Judge Severus would like to talk to you about Atalanta," said Vulso. "You may be able to provide him with information he needs."

"I don't know what information that can be. But let me change into something more appropriate for appearing before a judge and I'll be right with you."

She went into the next room and came out a about a half hour later dressed in a pale pink tunic with a soft yellow belt. A purple amethyst necklace and an amethyst bracelet complemented her appearance. Her face and eyes were made up and she projected a slight look of helplessness. She looked appealing, like a woman in need of rescue. Vulso knew that Severus would immediately respond favorably to her and she was undoubtedly aware of the impression she would make.

In another half an hour they arrived at Judge Severus' chambers in the Forum of Augustus and Marilla was ushered directly into the judge's presence. Vipsania was asked to wait outside in the anteroom. Severus was seated behind his desk reading a scroll when Vulso showed her in. Alexander and court clerk Proculus sat with him. Severus politely stood up and introduced himself and his aides to Marilla when she came in.

"What are you reading, *eminentissime*?" Marilla ventured to ask the judge, as she sat down, presenting a touch of boldness along with helplessness.

Severus was always impressed by anyone asking him what he was reading because he loved to tell people what it was, hoping it would lead into a discussion of books or literature or history, if possible.

"Some letters of Seneca, one of my favorite authors."

"I don't know him that well," she replied.

"He's definitely worth reading and perhaps sometime I will tell you why. But now we have some business of importance to discuss. Namely your former *domina*, Atalanta."

"I will be glad to tell you whatever I know."

"How long had you been her slave?"

"For about seven years. I was her *ornatrix*. When her previous *ornatrix* died in the plague that ravaged the City then, she bought me from a friend who needed money. My daily duty was to apply her makeup, dab on her perfume, arrange her hair, help her choose her clothes and jewelry, and do all the things necessary to make her beauty shine. To make her alluring, a desirable courtesan, or achieve whatever effect she wanted to convey."

"Did you get along well with Atalanta?"

"I was her slave. I had to get along with her. And mostly she was caring of me, but it sometimes happened she was harsh with me. That was because sometimes she was one woman and sometimes another. When she was in a good mood, we got along well. When she was in a bad mood, she sometimes slapped me, but she never had me whipped and never molested me."

"Were you with her when she was the courtesan to General Crispinus and later when she left him and went with the painter Pictor?"

"Yes. When she bought me, she was living with the General. I followed her, of course, when she went to live with Pictor. Though she gave up being a courtesan, she always wanted an *ornatrix.*"

"Why did she go to live with Pictor and give up being a courtesan?"

"She was fed up with being a courtesan. She wanted her own life. She wanted to break free from the domination of her mother, who kept her plying the life of a courtesan. And she also wanted to break free from the men who kept her. So when Pictor fell for her like a cockroach into a basin, as they say, she took the opportunity and quit working. Instead, she saw the opportunity to become a painter, something she said always had wanted to do, even as a child. So she did it."

"When she became an artist, did you accompany her to various places where she made paintings?"

"Yes. When she took up painting, I was still her *ornatrix*, but I also had a new task, which was to carry her easel and her chair. She liked to carry her own paintbox."

"Did you go with her to the Red faction stables to paint a horse?"

"Yes."

"Tell me what happened."

"We were taken to a horse, I forget its name, and she painted the horse. It belonged to the chariot driver Zephyrus, who had been to Pictor's studio for a portrait of himself, which *domina* painted. Then he said he wanted his horse in the picture and asked her to come to the stables to paint the animal. I came with her, carrying her chair and easel, as usual. While she was working on the portrait of the horse, Zephyrus came by and suggested I could go, that he would have a slave carry her painting equipment back when she left. Atalanta agreed and I left. That's all I saw."

"And later, when Atalanta came home?"

"I don't know what happened exactly. But she was furious for days. She took it out on everyone. Yelled at Pictor, yelled at me, yelled at Maro and Glaukon, Pictor's assistants. Finally, she calmed down, but barely. I'm sure she told Pictor what had happened, but she never told me. I still don't know. Do you know?"

"Yes. She was raped by Zephyrus."

"Well, that explains her behavior."

"Did you accompany Atalanta when she went to paint the portrait of a shoemaker named Pedo in his shop?"

"Yes. As usual I carried her easel and chair and waited with her while she worked on the painting."

"Did she choose him because he was her shoemaker? Did she buy her shoes from him?"

"Oh no. I mean she sometimes bought shoes from him, but she knew him from the past. They knew each other well. I think she was once his courtesan."

"Pedo's courtesan? How could a shoemaker afford an expensive courtesan like Atalanta?"

"Because Pedo wasn't always a shoemaker. In fact, while she was painting him, she made sarcastic comments about him to me. It was rather cruel of her. She would say to me while painting him, 'Did you know Pedo grew up the son of a poor shoemaker? Did you know he got himself an education and then became an important member of the government'? Or, 'did you know, he once virtually ruled the province of Bithynia? But look at him now.' Or, 'did you know he was once wealthy, but had all his money and property confiscated by the Senate?'"

"He was sitting right there, wasn't he? He heard all this. So what did he say?"

"Nothing. He just sat there stoically, working on shoes, looking dejected, and took it as she hurled these taunts at him. 'He started as a shoemaker', she would say, 'and ended up a shoemaker. That's fate for you.' And she would stare at him and say, 'they blamed it on you and you took the rap for them, didn't you?' He just sat there working on his shoes, his face fixed, rigid and sullen. He never said a word. He suffered her taunts.

"But then, when she had finished painting and we were packing up her brushes and paints, she broke down and began to cry. I had never seen her do that. She ran to Pedo and threw her arms around him, sobbing, saying she was sorry for what she had said. Over and over again she cried she was sorry. I quickly gathered up her painting equipment and went out the door to wait outside. I thought it was a lovers' quarrel and wanted no part of it."

"How long did you wait?"

"About half an hour or so. Then Atalanta came out, her hair and clothes disheveled, and told me I could go home. She then went back inside."

Severus, Vulso, Alexander and Proculus all looked at each other in amazement as Marilla told her story. The shoemaker Pedo, once a wealthy government official, whose property had been confiscated by the Senate? What was that all about?

"What more do you know about this," Severus asked Marilla. "Do you know when Atalanta and Pedo had been together? Do you know anything about the Senate confiscating his property?"

"I've told you everything I know. I hope it helps you."

"It certainly will. Thank you, Marilla. You can go now."

"That sheds a whole new light on matters, doesn't it?" said Severus rhetorically, the moment she was gone. "First, we have to find out about Pedo's past."

"If he had his property confiscated by the Senate," said Proculus, "that means there must have been a trial before the Senate. And since trials before the Senate almost always involve Senators as defendants, and since Pedo was not a Senator...'

"Since Pedo was not a Senator," Alexander took up the thought, "someone else, a Senator, was the main defendant and from that remark of Atalanta, Pedo somehow took the rap for him."

"She mentioned the province of Bithynia," added Vulso. "Therefore, it may be that the trial before the Senate was a trial for *repetundae*, extortion by the governor of the province. And if Pedo once virtually ruled the province, he was probably someone assisting the Propraetor, a *comes*, one of his staff of *comites*,"

"Sounds right," said Proculus. "And I remember there was a trial in the Senate maybe ten years ago concerning the province of Bithynia. The trial was of the Propraetor for extorting money from the province. Bithynia is a Senatorial province, not an Imperial province where the Emperor appoints a Prefect as governor. So the Senate appointed Bithynia's governor and naturally the provincials would bring charges against the governor to the Senate. And I know the governor's name too. It's on the tip of my tongue. I must be getting old. I used to know these things at the snap of a finger. His name is, his name is.... Oh, yes. Now I remember. It was Scapula. Septimius Scapula."

"Yes," added Severus. "I remember that case too. Septimius Scapula was tried before the Senate for extortion. But what happened? I don't remember. Does anyone remember?"

"No," said Proculus, "I don't. There was a trial. That I know. But I don't know the outcome."

"Alexander, go to the Tabularium archives and find the records of a trial for extortion by the governor of Bithynia, Septimius Scapula. See if someone named Pedo is mentioned. And if so, if he was also on trial, find out who was his lawyer. I want to talk to him. And also get the name of the prosecutor. If the province brought charges against a Senator in the Senate, it may well be that the Senate appointed the prosecutor. Whatever the trial record shows us will be important, of course. But we'll get the full story from the lawyers for the prosecution and defense. They will know things that are not in the transcripts.

That evening, Vulso sent a message to his two concubines at home, saying that he had to go out of Rome for the night on a mission for Judge Severus. At the same time, Vipsania told her grandmother that she would be staying with a friend for the night. Then, as Vulso and Vipsania had conspired that afternoon while she was taking him to find Marilla, they met at the Athena's Mantle Hotel on a side street off Public Swimming Pool Street, near the Ostia Gate. It was a hotel where Vulso had once terrorized its owner during the investigation of the case of the body found on the steps of the Temple of Mars the Avenger. Since then, Vulso was given the best room in the place whenever he wanted it, for free, no questions asked. And so, he exercised his perk for a night with Vipsania.

It was a stimulating, enjoyable, lascivious night for both of them.

SCROLL III

XIII

A TRIAL IN THE SENATE

"I'll tell you what happened at the trial," said Persephone, Alexander's wife, at breakfast the next morning.

They were eating olives and bread with honey and drinking milk. Persephone and Alexander had been married barely six months, having met during Judge Severus' last *cognitio* concerning the robbery of silk from the merchant ship *Andromeda*. They were both ex-slaves who had been freed, and each was still working for their previous owners as private secretaries. Alexander had been seduced by Persephone after they first met and was still seduced, not just by her beauty, but by her intelligence. He was madly in love with her. She appreciated his intellect and vast store of knowledge and loved him in return. She had never met anyone like him. His talk and thoughts were always stimulating. But even more, it was his sweet and unassuming character she loved most.

"How can you know what happened? You haven't seen the trial record, as I'm going to do in a few hours at the Tabularium."

"It's a trial in the Senate of a senator, along with a non-senator aide, is that right?"

"Yes."

Her manner became sardonic. "Don't you know these people by now? We have both been slaves. These upper-class elitists, with a few exceptions like your Judge Severus, stick together. If it comes to assigning guilt, no matter what the truth is, they are innocent. Everyone lower in status is guilty. That's the real nature of the society we live in. That's why trials of senators are held in the Senate, isn't it? So this governor Scapula will be found innocent, and his aide Pedo guilty. That's my prediction."

"Maybe so," answered Alexander. "But there have been famous cases where senators were prosecuted by other senators and found guilty by the Senate. Cicero's famous prosecution of Verres, the governor of Sicily, almost 250 years ago is a famous example. More recently the prosecution led by both Tacitus and Pliny the Younger convicted the then Propraetor of Bithynia of extortion. And there have been others as well." Alexander thought it over another moment. "But, you're right of course, some senators get very lenient treatment from their senatorial colleagues. Not a surprise, exactly." He stood up from the table and kissed her. "I'm off to the Tabularium. I'll have more to tell you when I get home tonight."

At the 3rd hour, Alexander arrived at the Tabularium building where the state archives were kept. The Tabularium had three stories above ground and a large basement substructure beneath. It was situated at the north end of the Old Forum at the foot of the Capitoline Hill, commanding a sweeping view over the Old Forum.

Alexander was not there for the view. Accompanied by three slaves of the Court of the Urban Prefect, he was there to search for a record of the trial in the Senate of Septimius Scapula, about 10 years earlier. Fortunately, no long search was needed. The clerks at the Tabularium were fully conversant with the recent archives and where they were located.

"Our records of Senate trials go back hundreds of years," informed a tall, thin, bony clerk in an ordinary gray tunic. Whether he was a slave or a freedman or just a free born Roman citizen, could not be told from his dress or manner. "But those records are stored deep in the basement. Recent Senate archives are here on the 2nd or 3rd floor. What trial are you looking for?"

"I don't know the year exactly, but it was a trial for extortion of the Propraetor of Bithynia named Septimius Scapula."

"Oh yes, I remember that trial. A very interesting case. I've actually read through some of the transcript because, after all, what else do I have to do here among old archives."

Alexander presented a document to the clerk. "This is an order from the *Iudex Selectus* Marcus Flavius Severus for that trial record and for permission to remove the records temporarily as part of an official investigation."

He handed a papyrus document to the clerk, who read it over.

"Of course, we usually don't permit official state archives to be removed, but with a court order, that's something else. Follow me."

The clerk led Alexander and the three slaves along a corridor and up a staircase and then down two more corridors to a far wall with a stack of floor to ceiling cubby-hole cases, each cubby-hole containing a substantial number of scrolls. Red label tags hung from the ends of the scrolls. A tall ladder on wheels gave access to the higher levels of the stack.

"This is where the recent Senate trial transcripts are stored. By recent I mean within the last 50 years or so. Just look through the tags and you'll find the case you're looking for. Then bring me the scrolls you want and I'll check them out for you."

Alexander thanked him and he and the slaves began looking through the red label tags, dividing the areas among them. One of the slaves sprawled on the ground examining lower-level labels, while another climbed the ladder to look at upper-level labels. Alexander and the third slave examined midlevel labels.

"A lot of trials," commented one of the slaves.

"Yes," confirmed Alexander. "A lot of senators needed to be put on trial."

"I wonder how many were acquittals," commented another of the slaves. "After all, it was the Senate trying senators. I'll bet most of them got off."

"I've found it," said the slave high up on the ladder. "All the scrolls in this cubby-hole have labels designating the Senate trial of Septimius Scapula *et al.*"

"Hand them down," said Alexander. "And let's look at them. We want especially to see whether someone named Pedo was one of the others on trial, and generally what the trial was all about. And the verdicts, of course."

The slave started handing down scrolls, which another slave took to a table nearby. Alexander seated himself and began to organize the scrolls by their labels and then started with a quick scan of their contents. When he was done organizing, Alexander told the others that they would have to take all the scrolls.

"It looks like it was a typical 3-day Senate trial. As usual the defense got half as much time again as the prosecution, 6 hours for the prosecutor, 9 hours for the defense on the water clock. On the first day the prosecutor started off with his case and a defense attorney followed with his defense. On day two, the defense lawyer started, followed by the prosecutor, and then a defense rebuttal. On the third day there was testimony of witnesses and then summations and a verdict by the senators who voted by walking to one side of the House or the other."

"Was Pedo one of the defendants?" asked one of the slaves. "And what were the verdicts?" asked another.

Alexander unrolled the last scroll containing the verdicts. "The trial was of the Propraetor Scapula and two of his aides, Quintus Mucius and Gaius Pedo. As governor of Bithynia, Scapula was, of course, also the chief magistrate of the province. The three were prosecuted for taking bribes to convict an innocent person and acquit the guilty one. The bribe in this case was a million sesterces. Scapula denied he did anything wrong. He claimed he convicted only guilty defendants and acquitted the innocent. Mucius backed him up. They both blamed Pedo for taking bribes on his own and he was found guilty. All Pedo's property was confiscated and he was exiled from Rome for five years." So Persephone was right, Alexander immediately thought.

"So the lower class defendant took the rap," said one of the slaves, reaching the same conclusion as Persephone.

"That may be the case. But maybe the verdict was correct, maybe not. Maybe all three were guilty, including Pedo. Maybe the other two were guilty and Pedo innocent. We don't know the details yet. We'll have to read the transcript of the trial and probably talk to the lawyers. Pedo's lawyer in particular."

Alexander rose and told the slaves to put the scrolls into a round *capsa* carrying case and bring them to the Tabularium clerk to record their removal. When that was done, Alexander thanked the clerk for his help and turned to the slaves with him.

"Now back to Judge Severus' chambers. I'm sure he'll want to go over this transcript in detail."

When Alexander brought the trial transcripts back to Severus' chambers, the judge, his court clerk Proculus, his assessor Flaccus, and Alexander began to pore over the contents. What were the arguments of the lawyers? What was the evidence?

The first scrolls covered day one of the trial. The prosecutor, a senator named Tiberius Sosius Tertullus, had been appointed by the Senate to make the case against all three defendants together – Scapula and his two aides, Quintus Mucius and Gaius Pedo. The prosecutor made a good speech attacking the lead defendant, Septimius Scapula, the Propraetor of Bithynia. The accusation was that Scapula had accepted bribes to render unjust verdicts in cases before his court. In particular, Tertullus charged, a citizen of Bithynia, a merchant named Cleomedes had been strangled to death. The main suspect was his business partner, a Roman citizen named Manilius Rufus. The murdered man's family attested to violent arguments over money between the two leading up to the murder. There were also witnesses who put Rufus at the place where Cleomedes was murdered at the time of the killing. The case came before Scapula as governor of the province. He acquitted Rufus after a brief trial. The family of the murdered man claimed Rufus had bribed the judge with a million sesterces to acquit him. The money wasn't directly paid to Scapula, but instead was given to his aides, two of his *comites*, named Mucius and Pedo, who passed the money on to Scapula.

In the trial before the Senate, Scapula's lawyer did not dispute that a bribe was paid, but claimed that Scapula never received any bribe. He argued that Pedo had extorted the money from Rufus' family and kept it for himself. How else, argued Scapula's lawyer, did Pedo have so much money of his own, a fact that could not be disputed. The prosecutor in the Senate replied convincingly that Rufus' guilt was clear, and that Scapula would never have acquitted him unless Scapula himself had been bribed. As to Pedo's wealth, it was irrelevant to Scapula's guilt. Finally, in the summation before the Senate, Scapula's lawyer emphasized that Scapula was a Roman senator and Pedo a lower-class upstart who had advanced to the governor's staff by lying and trickery and manipulation. He was the extortioner, not the honorable governor of the province.

Scapula's defense was backed up by another aide, Quintus Mucius, who was also a defendant in this trial. He claimed he was innocent and had never taken any bribe. However, he said he happened to see Rufus' son give Pedo the bribe money. Pedo's lawyer denied any of it, pointing out that Mucius was Scapula's son-in-law and his testimony was not to be trusted.

The defense witnesses were Scapula, Mucius and Pedo, each asserting their claims of innocence, but with Scapula and Mucius accusing Pedo of taking bribes.

The main witness for the prosecution was son of the murdered man Cleomedes, who testified it was notorious that Scapula extorted money from many provincials for favorable verdicts. He had heard not just about favorable verdicts. Scapula also took bribes to give out government jobs, government contracts, and other legal decisions. The *modus operandi* in all this corruption was to have Scapula's aides, Mucius and Pedo, solicit and collect bribes on the understanding that Scapula would render the decision the briber wanted. Bribes were paid and acquittals, jobs, contracts and favorable legal rulings were rendered. But no one else from Bithynia other than the son of Cleomedes appeared at the trial, whether because it was just too onerous to travel so far or because of threats or bribes to stay away. It was not known which.

As a result, when the Senate was asked to divide on the guilt of Scapula, two out of three senators walked to Scapula's side of the House to vote him innocent. When it was time to divide on the guilt or innocence of Mucius and Pedo, Mucius was acquitted and Pedo convicted.

Pedo's sentence was confiscation of all his property and exile for five years. This was considered a light penalty because he easily could have been exiled for life. But with the loss of his rank, his property and his return to meager beginnings, he went, as the saying goes, from the sky into the mud.

"I see that Pedo's lawyer is named Gaius Papirius," observed Severus. "Tomorrow, I want to see him. I also want to talk to the prosecutor, Tertullus. Let's get the full story."

That night Alexander returned home and at dinner told Persephone that she was right. The senator was acquitted and his lower-class aide convicted. Persephone just smiled knowingly, and took Alexander to bed.

XIV

PROSECUTION AND DEFENSE LAWYERS TALK ABOUT THE TRIAL

The next morning at the 4th hour, the prosecutor Senator Tertullus, appeared in Severus' chambers following an exchange of messages. Alexander and Vulso sat in on the interview. Tertullus was dressed in formal senatorial clothes, with a bright white toga and a tunic that displayed the broad reddish-purple stripe of the Senatorial Order. He was an imposing looking man, somewhat corpulent, with intelligent brown eyes and an easy-going manner. But when talk turned to the Scapula case, his manner became grim and angry.

"*Eminentissime*, there's no doubt in my mind that Scapula, Mucius and Pedo were all guilty. They blamed it on Pedo alone, which was unjust. Pedo was guilty of conspiring with them, but he wasn't the lone culprit. They were all in it together. One was more devious than the other. It was rare for Scapula to personally take a bribe. He left it to Mucius and Pedo to collect. Both were intimidating, Mucius because of his sinister manner and Pedo because he was big and strong. I believed then and I still believe now that they were all working together to rob the province. They shared the loot, although undoubtedly Scapula got the largest share."

"How did you come to that conclusion, *clarissime*?" asked Severus, careful to return the senatorial encomium in return for Tertullus' use of the equestrian honorific.

"As a witness Scapula wasn't bad. He was a smooth liar, but still a liar. His story didn't hold water. I examined the underlying facts of the murder and Rufus was obviously guilty. He was therefore wrongfully acquitted. Bribery was the only way to explain that verdict.

"As for the governor's aide Mucius, he even smirked while telling his phony story backing Scapula and laying the blame on Pedo. Maybe it's understandable that he was lying for his father-in-law, but his manner was shifty and his story too convenient, not worth a tuft of wool, as the saying goes.

"Anyway, why this sudden interest in Pedo? The trial was more than ten years ago.:

"Pedo has been murdered and I've been appointed by the Urban Prefect to find his murderer as well as the killer of two others whose murder is linked to his."

"I didn't know he was murdered. Too bad. Who are the two others?"

"A chariot driver for the Reds named Zephyrus and a courtesan named Atalanta."

"I was hoping you would say Scapula and Mucius. If Pedo deserves to be murdered, they all do. But I've never heard of either of the victims you named, not being a fan of the Circus or a devotee of courtesans."

"One other question, Senator Tertullus." Severus nodded to Alexander who picked up a scroll and unrolled it, displaying the face of the unidentified man painted by Atalanta. "Do you happen to recognize him, *clarissime*?"

"No, *eminentissime*. I do not."

In the afternoon, Pedo's lawyer, Gaius Papirius, came into Severus' chambers. Like Severus, he was a member of the Equestrian Order and wore his toga over a tunic displaying a narrow stripe. When Severus explained that he wanted to know about Pedo and the Senate trial, Papirius gave a wry smile.

"You want to know about Pedo, *eminentissime*? I'll tell you the real story. Do you know how the son of a shoemaker came to be one of the *comites* of a Roman Propraetor?"

Severus shook his head negatively.

"Do you know about General Pertinax, who started out as the son of a freed slave?"

"I know that Pertinax is one of the top Generals in the Imperium, thought very highly of by the Emperor. Why do you ask?"

"Because Pedo's story is connected with Pertinax. This is what happened. Pertinax, as you may know, is the son of a freed slave. As a youth, Pertinax received a good education and became a grammarian, teaching Latin and Greek grammar and literature, Homer and Virgil. When he was in his 30's Pertinax decided to switch careers and through an influential friend wangled an appointment as a centurion in the legions."

Severus understood that process personally, since he himself had wangled an appointment for his son Aulus as a legionary Tribune through his friendship and influence with the Emperor.

Papirius continued. "Pertinax' natural talent and hard work contributed to his rise in the army. He won praise and success during the recent war with Parthia. This led to promotions. He became a Tribune and now is the Legatus, the commanding General of the Legion I Adiutrix, currently fighting on the German frontier with the Emperor.

"What does this have to do with Pedo? Well, when Pedo was growing up he had been a student of Pertinax, who was then still teaching. Later, when Pertinax went into the army, he took with him a number of talented former students as his trusted aides. One of them was Pedo. He became a confidante of Pertinax and rose to the rank of military Tribune. At some point, when Pertinax switched assignments, Pedo joined the staff of Septimius Scapula, when he became the governor of Bithynia. But while Pertinax was honest and trustworthy, Scapula was dishonest and corrupt. I believe Scapula corrupted Pedo."

"Do you believe Pedo was guilty of taking bribes in Bithynia?"

"Yes. I believe it. He was from a poor shoemaker family. I think he couldn't resist the money and the power and everything that goes with becoming rich. How many people could resist? In this sense, I believe he was a victim of Scapula's corruption as much as a beneficiary of it. Pedo became rich by going along with the corrupt governor he was working for. When he returned to Rome, he bought a *domus* for himself, along with slaves. He lived high and mighty. Where did all that money come from? Obviously from corruption during his time on Scapula's staff in Bithynia. But he was certainly not alone. Scapula was the instigator of various corrupt schemes, taking advantage of his power as governor, and he used both Pedo and his son-in-law Mucius as his henchmen. Pedo certainly profited handsomely from the corruption of Scapula. But though he was an accomplice in Scapula's crimes, Pedo was thrown to the lions by Scapula when the time came for assigning blame. Then Scapula wormed out of it and thrust the full guilt on Pedo. Pedo was convicted, exiled, all his property confiscated. He was ruined.

"To achieve this result, it was not exactly irrelevant that both Scapula and his son-in-law Mucius are members of the Senatorial Order. Pedo was not even an Equestrian. He was just an up-start lower class freedman, one of the *vulgi*. The son of a freed slave. From making shoes he came, to making shoes he returned."

"Do you know that Pedo has been murdered?"

"No. I didn't know. Who killed him and why?"

"That's my *cognitio*, to find out who killed him and two others in a manner associated with the death of Pedo. One was a chariot driver for the Reds, Zephyrus, and the other a courtesan, Atalanta."

"I heard that Zephyrus died, but I thought it was in an accident in the Circus Maximus."

"That was the story that was put out by the Red faction, but actually he was murdered. And Atalanta? Do you know of her by any chance?"

"Atalanta? Of course. She was Pedo's courtesan for a few years, before and during the time of his trial in the Senate. She supported him and she was often present when I was with Pedo preparing his case. I would say, though, that she was more than just his courtesan. They were in love with each other. Unfortunately, they had a falling out after he was convicted and lost everything and went into exile. He wanted her to go into exile with him, but she refused and left him. Who murdered her? Why? She was a very beautiful and talented woman."

"I'm trying to find the answer to that as well. Who murdered the three of them."

"What makes you think those three murders are connected?"

"The killer wrote the number 'I' in blood on the cheek of the first victim, Zephyrus, the number 'II' on the cheek of the second victim, Atalanta, and the number 'III' on the cheek of the third, Pedo. Also there was the same method used to lure all three victims to their deaths. Each received a tablet with an erotic love poem of Catullus, each responded by immediately going out to meet the sender. Then each was murdered in the same way, with their throats cut. And the three murders occurred on three days in a row, an unlikely coincidence unless they were connected."

"Pedo was connected with Atalanta, as I told you, but I don't know that he had any connection with this Zephyrus or even had any interest in chariot racing.

So I can't help you there. Out of curiosity, where was Pedo killed?"

"He was found where he worked and lived at the foot of his bed, his throat cut."

"Someone must have taken him by surprise from behind then. He was no weakling and would not be an easy man to kill otherwise."

"You've helped me, Papirius. I didn't know that Atalanta was once Pedo's courtesan. And even more than that, they were lovers. That sheds new light on matters. So thank you. But before you leave, I have one more question. Severus nodded to Alexander who picked up a scroll and unrolled it, displaying the face of the unidentified man painted by Atalanta. "Do you happen to recognize this man?"

"Sorry, *eminentissime,* I never saw him before in my life."

XV

A SYMPOSIUM ON THE CASE

That evening, Severus invited his whole staff to his house for dinner. The plan was to have a good meal and then a good discussion about where they were in the case. What they had learned, what their theories were, and how they should proceed. A symposium about the case, as it was so far.

Before dinner, Artemisia told Severus there would be another guest for dinner.

"Who is that?"

"Publius Flamma, Aulus' army friend. He and Flavia met in the park this afternoon and played cithara music together and got to know each other."

"How did it go?"

"Very well. Very well, indeed. According to Aulus, Flamma instantly fell for Flavia. "

"And Flavia? How does she feel about him?"

"She likes him, she told me later. But she says she's confused. She was positive that she would never want to be with anyone again after Bellerephon. But after playing music together with Flamma, she's not so certain anymore. She admitted he appeals to her, but right now only as a friend. She's willing to see more of him. Play more music. Talk about poetry. So I've invited him to dinner this evening."

"Fine. Maybe it will work out between Flavia and Flamma. If not? That's life."

The dinner was catered by a local taberna and a traditional meal 'from eggs to apples' was ordered for their enjoyment. Usually, a *triclinium* dining room had three dinner couches, holding the traditional nine people for a traditional dinner party. However, this evening a fourth couch was set up around the low dining table because there were twelve diners, not nine.

On the head couch were Severus, Artemisia and their daughter Flavia. On the couch to the right of the dining table were the judge's police aides Vulso and Straton and his bodyguard Crantor, while his court clerk Proculus, his private secretary Alexander and his former assessor Flaccus occupied the third couch on the left of the dining table.

Aulus, was on another couch, across the table from the head couch, along with his younger brother Quintus and Publius Flamma. While Aulus and Quintus were concentrating on the food as it came, Flamma couldn't take his eyes off Flavia, across the table. She, with some subtlety, met his fixation with fleeting inviting looks.

The twelve diners on four couches engaged in various animated conversations with their couch neighbors when Tryphon, one of the family slaves, brought in incense, lit it and intoned a traditional invocation to the gods. None of these formalities interfered with any of the conversations, but the talking stopped momentarily when the first dish was brought in -- soft boiled eggs with pepper, honey, vinegar and pine-kernels.

At the same time, two musicians entered the triclinium, sat down on chairs, and began to play, one on a 12-string lyre and the other on a 7-string cithara. It was music supposedly meant to stimulate digestion and enjoyment of food. Whether it actually did so was debatable, but it was not debatable that the music was a pleasant accompaniment to dining.

Milk-fed snails with wine and salty *liquamen* preceded the main course -- duck with turnips in a sauce of cumin, coriander and pepper. The dessert was apples dipped in honey.

The wine was a good white Falernian.

As the dinner wound down, the musicians were asked to wait in the atrium, and the topic of murder started up.

"I want to discuss," began Severus, "where we are in the investigation and where we go next, so I'll review a bit. We have three murders in three days. The first was Zephyrus, a chariot driver for the Red faction, then Atalanta, a courtesan, and lastly Pedo, a shoemaker. Zephyrus and Atalanta were each lured out of their homes by receiving a tablet with a love poem by Catullus. Pedo had a Catullus tablet in his home, the place where he was found dead. All were killed by having their throats cut with a dagger. The first victim, Zephyrus had the number 'I' written on his cheek, Atalanta had the number 'II' on her cheek, and Pedo the number 'III'. The numbers were written in the blood of the victims, presumably by the murderer dipping his finger in the blood gushing from the slit throats."

"It's a good thing," interrupted Flaccus, "that you're telling this to us after dinner, not before."

Severus smiled and continued. "We have learned about Atalanta, that she was a courtesan who had for a time given it up and lived with a painter named Pictor. She herself took up painting and became an accomplished portrait painter. We know she painted a portrait of the charioteer Zephyrus and when she went to the Red stables to paint his horse, he lured her into his room and raped her.

"We also know that she had once been the courtesan of Pedo, who was at that time not a shoemaker as he had been as a boy, but had risen to become a *comes* in the retinue of the governor of Bithynia, Septimius Scapula. Scapula, along with Pedo and another aide, his son-in-law Mucius, were tried before the Senate for extorting money from the provincials he was supposed to govern honestly and honorably. At the trial in the Senate, Scapula and Mucius were acquitted, but Pedo was convicted after his co-defendants turned on him and claimed Pedo took bribes, but not themselves. Pedo had all his property confiscated and went into exile for five years.

"Presumably, then, all three were killed by the same person, a nemesis, whose name and reason for the crimes we don't know. And presumably, the killer knew all three, and the victims had something in common that led to their deaths. Moreover, what we know about the killer is very little. But the act of putting the number I on the first victim implies that there will be a second victim. So we can conclude that the murder of Zephyrus was connected to the murder of Atalanta. And then of Pedo. Also, the fact that the three murders were committed in three days, one after the other, suggests a connection in the murderer's mind. But what is the connection?"

Alexander spoke up. "We have Atalanta connected to Zephyrus and Pedo, she painted them both and had sex with both, forcibly with Zephyrus and voluntarily with Pedo, as master and courtesan, as lovers. But having victim II connected to I and III, we don't know whether and how I is connected to III. But is Zephyrus connected directly to Pedo? We haven't closed the circle, so to speak."

"If there is a circle to close?" spoke up Flaccus. "Only the murderer knows why he killed those three. Maybe I and III didn't know each other at all, but maybe all three knew something that the killer wanted kept quiet."

"Like what?" asked Artemisia.

"I don't know," replied Flaccus. "Maybe it was something that killer did that they knew about. A crime, perhaps."

"Could be," replied Artemisia. "After all, Pedo knew about wrongs committed by Scapula, the governor of Bithynia. And Pedo could well have told his courtesan Atalanta about them. And it's likely that Scapula's crimes weren't just confined to extortion in the one case of an unjust verdict that came before the Senate. Probably there were others, even lots of others. And maybe there were extortions of the provincials not only in legal matters, but in giving out contracts, government jobs. Isn't that what corrupt Roman governors do? Isn't that what the provincials claimed he did? Wasn't there even testimony about that in the prosecutor's case before the Senate?"

"You have a good point there," responded Severus. "So if we assume that Scapula committed other crimes that Pedo knew about and told Atalanta about, that may provide a good reason to silence them. But then how does Zephyrus fit in?"

Alexander interjected. "Maybe one of those crimes involved chariot racing. In that case we have to go back to the Red faction and see if Scapula's name shows up there."

"Good idea," replied Severus. "I'll summon the *dominus* of the faction, Gordianus, to my chambers tomorrow.

"Quintus, send Gordianus a message. And also, let's talk to that assistant of his Nicias, who seems to know things, and Paris, a lover of Zephyrus. If I remember correctly, when we first talked to them at the stables, I specifically asked whether they knew a courtesan named Atalanta and they said only that the faction was deluged with women and they didn't know their names. But later we learned that Atalanta was at the stables to paint Zephyrus' horse, that he raped her, and that he bragged about it. Therefore, Nicias knew about Atalanta, though perhaps he didn't know her name, although maybe he did. The others must have heard about the Zephyrus rape as well. So Nicias possibly lied to us, and maybe so did Gordianus and Paris. I want them all in my chambers tomorrow. This time I'll question them in my lair, not in theirs."

"I'll send out messages first thing in the morning."replied Proculus. "We'll order them to come after lunch. At the 9th hour, say."

"Good. And then it seems we should follow up on Scapula. He or his son-in-law Mucius or both might have wanted Pedo and Atalanta silenced to cover up their crimes. Maybe Pedo was trying to extort money from them to keep silent. So they are suspects."

"But here's something else to consider," said Artemisia. "The love poems, the ones that lured all three to their deaths. Each must have been willing, even eager, to meet the sender of the poem. Each must have known immediately who sent it to them and who they were going to meet, and probably the meeting was expected to be for love or sex. Do Scapula or his son-in-law fit that requirement? I haven't seen them, but probably not. And we don't even know whether the lover each victim met was a man or a woman. It could be either."

"You're right about that, *deliciae,*" replied Severus. "But we have to resume the investigation somewhere. And we have two good places to resume. With the three liars from the Red faction in my chambers tomorrow, and then with Scapula and Mucius next. I'm going to put pressure on all of them and see what we can squeeze out."

"Haven't you forgotten something?" spoke up Vulso.

"What's that?"

"The unidentified man painted by Atalanta. Who is he? We don't know. Everyone we've showed the painting to says they don't recognize him. That's Pictor, General Crispinus, Atalanta's family, Pedo's prosecutor and his lawyer. Maybe he is the murderer. Who knows?"

"We didn't have that portrait when we first went to the Red faction stables. I'll show it to them when I interview them tomorrow.

"So now, let's call back the musicians, have some more wine, and finish off our symposium with good cheer and good hopes."

They all stayed to listen to the music and drink more wine except for Flavia and Flamma. They left the symposium and walked off together.

Later that night, Severus and Artemisia lay in bed discussing things.

"This may be a very good development," said Artemisia. "Flavia and Flamma, I mean. She's not as enthusiastic about him as he is with her, but maybe it will work out."

"It certainly is good news. It may solve Flavia's problem, turn her life around."

"Yes, *deliciae*. But while this is good news about Flavia, I have bad news about Aulus."

"Aulus? What's wrong?"

"He says he wants to see action. There's a war going on with the Germans on the Danube and he wants to be part of it. He complains that all he's doing as an Equestrian Tribune are legionary financial accounts in Cappadocia where nothing is happening. He wants to transfer to a legion that's fighting a real war. He says real Romans want to fight, not keep accounts."

"I see. And you want me to dissuade him. I can try, but Aulus is not a child and he can and will make his own decisions. If he decides he wants to go to the front and fight in a war, I don't know if I can stop him."

"Talk to him, at least. Fighting Germans? He must be out of his mind."

Severus shrugged. "I'll see what I can do." To himself, however, he felt a certain pride in Aulus' desire to fight for Rome. He himself when he was younger had wanted to join the army, but instead pursued advanced studies in Athens. He didn't regret that decision. After all, that's where he had met Artemisia. But he always thought himself lacking in some way because he hadn't been in the army. Also, he realized that Artemisia, being a Greek, couldn't care less about Roman military exploits. If anything, she opposed them. So while he would talk to Aulus, as he promised his wife, and attempt to dissuade him from transferring to a dangerous war front, he secretly hoped Aulus wouldn't listen to him. It was logically wrong of him to feel this way, he knew. He should want his son to avoid danger, not court it. But just the same, Severus couldn't help having these feelings.

He had a hard time falling asleep.

XVI

THE RED FACTION COMES TO SEVERUS' CHAMBERS

"To be clear," said Severus to Vulso, Crantor and Alexander, They were with him in his chambers when the people from the Red faction were waiting in the anteroom. "We want to know two things. First, whether there was any connection between the charioteer Zephyrus and Pedo, the shoemaker, formerly *Comes* to the governor of Bithynia. Second, whether anyone can identify the unknown man in Atalanta's portrait."

"Who do we see first?" asked Vulso.

"The weakest. Paris. Zephyrus' sometime lover. That's why both of you, Vulso and Crantor, are here. I'll ask him things nicely at first. But if he is reluctant to be helpful, then intimidation is in order."

"How far can we take intimidation?" asked Crantor logically.

"As far as necessary," replied Severus vaguely. "Alexander, bring in Paris. You can tell both Gordianus and Nicias they have to wait."

Alexander went out and brought in Paris. When they had seen him at the Red faction stables, he had gold dust in his hair and a beautiful, almost feminine face and effeminate movements. Nothing had changed. Paris swished in with fresh gold dust in his hair and while he had an apprehensive look on his face, when he saw Vulso he gave him a sly smile. Vulso almost burst out laughing, but controlled himself.

"Sit down, Paris. I have a few questions to ask you," began the judge.

Paris took a seat. "I am at your service, *eminentissime*."

"Paris, when we talked to you at the Red faction stables not too long ago, we asked you whether you knew of a courtesan named Atalanta. You said you didn't. But, Paris, we now know that you weren't telling the truth."

"Me, not telling the truth, *eminentissime*?" He made a weak smile. "No. I told the truth."

Severus' voice hardened. "Paris, we know that Atalanta was at the stables to paint Zephyrus' horse and that then Zephyrus raped her. He bragged about it to everyone. Everyone knew. You must have known too. Right?"

"I knew he raped that woman painter. I didn't know her name, that's all. I wasn't lying."

"Well now you know her name. I want to know about the rape."

"I only know what Zephyrus told me. He teased me about the woman. He said he raped her and that she was better than me. I told him he could rape me anytime he wanted. He just laughed at me."

"What else did he say about Atalanta?"

"Nothing else."

"I'm not sure whether I believe you, Paris. You lied when you said you didn't know Atalanta. Therefore, I have to believe you also lied when you said you didn't know the shoemaker Pedo."

"I don't know any shoemaker Pedo."

"Suppose I tell you that this shoemaker Pedo was once a confidential aide to the governor of Bithynia, Septimius Scapula. Both were tried in the Senate. Do you know him now?"

"No. I never met any such person."

Severus gave him a hard look. "I want the truth, Paris."

"No, really, *eminentissime*. I never heard of this Pedo. I swear it. I swear by Jupiter and the stone."

"I want to know whether you know this man." He motioned to Alexander who unfurled the painting of the unidentified man. Paris looked at it and his eyes widened visibly, a surprised look on his face.

"No. I don't know him."

"From the way you looked just now when you saw his face, I think you do know him."

"No. No. I don't. I really don't."

"Don't swear by Jupiter and the stone this time. Jupiter wouldn't like it. I know I don't believe your denial." Severus got up and motioned to Alexander. They both left the room, leaving Paris alone with Vulso and Crantor.

"What will they do to him?" asked Alexander.

"Persuade him," replied Severus. "I remember once when investigating the shipwreck conspiracy, when Crantor persuaded someone by breaking his fingers, one by one. I don't know if he'll have to do that to Paris."

"But what if Paris really doesn't know?"

"You saw the look on his face when he saw the painting. He knows."

It wasn't long before Vulso came into the anteroom. "He now knows who the painting portrays."

Severus and Alexander walked back into his chambers. Severus took his seat behind his desk. Paris looked unharmed, but terrified. He used his handkerchief to wipe the sweat from his brow.

"Who is the man in the painting?" asked Severus.

"It's Claudius. Claudius Glabrio."

"Who is he?"

"A tout. He hangs around the stables. He tries to get information from the charioteers. You know, for betting on the races. He uses inside information for his own betting and sells it to other bettors."

"Was Zephyrus one of the charioteers he talked to?"

"Yes. Of course. He talked to anyone he could. Not just the drivers, but the stable hands also. He wants to know the condition of the horses as well as of the drivers."

"Where can we find this Claudius Glabrio?"

"I don't know. You can ask Nicias or Gordianus. He used to talk to them too. One of them might know. I don't."

"All right, Paris. You can go."

Paris bolted out, as fast as a chariot leaving the starting gate.

When he was gone, Alexander asked Vulso and Crantor what they did to him to make him talk like that.

"Nothing," replied Vulso. "We never even touched him."

Crantor laughed. "But we let him know what would happen if we did touch him."

Severus then commented to his aides in an upbeat manner. "Now we're getting somewhere. Now we want to know how Atalanta came to paint this Glabrio. She wasn't a hanger on at the Red stables, she only came here once, as far as we know. So how does she come to know Glabrio? What's the connection? Alexander, bring in both Gordianus and Nicias together."

Both Gordianus, the *dominus* of the faction and his top assistant Nicias came in. They both looked a bit miffed, apparently not liking that they were summoned to Severus' chambers in the first place and then that they were kept waiting while the judge talked to Paris.

Severus ignored their looks. He motioned to Alexander who showed them the painting.

"Tell us about him. About Claudius Glabrio."

"A tout," said Nicias. "He hangs around the stables like plenty of others, picking up information for bettors. He is a bettor himself and he also sells information to others for them to use in their bets."

"Where can I find him?"

"I don't know where he lives. But he's at one or the other stables almost every day. So he can be found at either the Greens stables, the Blues or the Whites, if he's not at ours."

Severus turned to Vulso and Crantor. "All the stables are near one another. So go to each of them, one by one, find Claudius Glabrio and bring him here."

They both left on the spot.

Severus continued to question both Gordianus and Nicias about whether they knew Pedo. Neither admitted to knowing him at all. He asked them about Atalanta and Zephyrus' rape. They both said they knew about Zephyrus raping the woman painter. Zephyrus bragged about it. But they never knew her name. They were told they could leave.

"What now?" asked Alexander.

"Now we wait for Vulso and Crantor to return, hopefully with the tout Glabrio. So let's play a game of *Latrunculi* until they return."

Alexander had been studying *Latrunculi,* hoping to become good enough to match up to the judge. Alexander was good at the game and had recently managed to draw a game with Severus. He was improving, particularly because Severus would replay their games with him and discuss and analyze them together. Severus was happy to improve Alexander's play to the point where their games would become competitive and interesting. And their games were getting to that point.

Alexander put an elegant oak board on the desk between them. The board was marked by black lines into 64 squares, 8 x 8. He held out his closed hands containing the *calculi,* one white and one black. Severus tapped the left hand and drew the white *calculus.* He would move first. Each then set up his men, one on each of the first 8 squares in front of him, and the pyramid shaped piece called *Dux* on the square in front of the other *calculi*, 5 squares in from the left.

Each *calculus* was made of glass, convex on top for easy handling. Each *calculus* moved forward, backwards or sideways any number of squares, but not diagonally. An opponent's piece could be captured by surrounding it on two opposite sides. If the *Dux* was surrounded on all four sides or on three sides and pinned against a side of the board on the fourth, the game would be won instantly by the attacker.

Latrunculi was strictly a game of thought. No dice were used. Players had to think ahead planning strategy and calculating tactics. At its best, *Latrunculi* was entertaining, fascinating, absorbing, clever, surprising in its constantly changing and myriad positions and full of ideas. It was a game, a sport, a competition, an interest, a world of its own. Severus was a master at it.

The game had progressed to a complicated middle-game position, full of possibilities when Vulso and Crantor returned with Claudius Glabrio in tow.

"We found him at the Greens stables," said Vulso.

"Bring him in," said the judge, as Alexander put the board on another table, the *calculi* in place for resuming the game.

Vulso went out into the anteroom and ushered in Claudius Glabrio.

XVII

GLABRIO, THE TOUT

Glabrio was a thin man with a scraggly beard, thin lips, darting eyes and large ears. He was less appealing to look at in person than in Atalanta's painting of him. Seated before the judge, he looked confused and frightened. He didn't know why he was there. An innate suspiciousness and fear of authority enhanced his discomfort. Had he done something wrong? Or had something questionable he had done been found out? He was scared.

Severus came straight to the point. "The painter Atalanta painted your portrait." Alexander unfurled it and showed it to Glabrio. "How did that come about?"

Glabrio looked relieved. Was this about a painting and not his touting?

"One day I was at a friend's place, *eminentissime*. She saw me there and wanted to paint me."

"Who is the friend?"

"His name is Pedo. He's a shoemaker. I sell him information about the chariot races. He's a client of mine."

So there it was, thought Severus. A connection between Zephyrus and Pedo and Atalanta. Glabrio knew them all. But what did it mean? Glabrio didn't seem to have any motive to kill his informant, Zephyrus, or his client, Pedo. Nor his painter Atalanta, for that matter. Nor did he seem to fit the role of a nemesis of the murder victims.

"I have a lot of questions for you, Glabrio. Do you want some wine? Some fruit?"

"Yes, *eminentissime.* I would like both." Glabrio took a deep breath. This might be enjoyable, he thought to himself. It might even be profitable. He smiled inwardly and outwardly, though still remaining somewhat wary. Wine and fruit were brought in and Glabrio grabbed some grapes and had a large quaff of wine.

"Let's talk about Pedo first. How do you know him?"

"As I said, he's a client. I sell him information about the chariot races. He told me he once was rich, lost his money, and wanted to become rich again. He thought betting on the races might be one way of making a lot of money. He always seems desperate for money. But, *eminentissime,* I haven't seen him for a while. He's no longer at his shoe shop. In fact, the shop is closed. I don't know where he is."

"What was Atalanta doing there? Was she painting him as well?"

"Not when I was there. She was just there. I think they were having an argument, though. When I came to the door, I heard them yelling at each other. They stopped when I came in to give him the latest news about the Circus. But a tense atmosphere was in the room. You could feel it. After that, as I left, they resumed yelling at each other."

"Did you hear what they were arguing about?"

"Not really. No. But I thought there was animosity between them. In the way of ex-lovers, like there had been a bad falling out. But the next time I went to Pedo's shop to give him news of the Circus, he said she was a painter and wanted to paint a portrait of me. I agreed to it and the next time I visited him, she was there with her paints and paint board."

"Was she alone? Didn't she have a slave or assistant with her to carry equipment?"

"Maybe she came with one, but when she was painting me, she was alone. Just Pedo was there."

"Did Pedo and Atalanta argue while you were being painted?"

"No. Actually they seemed to be talking to each other familiarly, like they were comfortable with each other. Like they were close. Intimate even."

"Now, you're a tout of chariot racing and you knew Zephyrus of the Red faction, didn't you?"

"Yes, *eminentissime*. I knew him. But he was killed. They say it happened in the races, but I know better. I know he was murdered. Too bad. I liked him. He gave me good information too."

"Did Zephyrus know Pedo?"

"I don't know for sure. But I met Pedo at the Red stables. He came around once or twice to try to get inside information for betting. He must have known someone, maybe Zephyrus, or paid someone off, to get into the stables in the first place. I told him that I did touting and I could get the kind of information he wanted and sell it to him cheaply. I told him I could even get better information than he could because, for one thing, I went to the stables of all four factions, and I went every day. He agreed and became my client. I brought him information at his shop and he didn't have to come to the stables. Anyway, I wouldn't be surprised if he and Zephyrus met because when Pedo came to the stables to get inside information, Zephyrus was someone he would naturally want to talk to. So yes, I believe they knew each other, but I don't know to what extent. Ask Pedo, if you can find him."

"Pedo is dead. Like Zephyrus. It's possible, even likely, that they were murdered by the same person. I'm trying to find that person. Atalanta was another victim of this killer as well."

"I didn't know that," replied Glabrio, looking aghast. "If I can help in any way, just ask."

"You knew Zephyrus, Atalanta and Pedo. Do you know of anyone else who knew them all?"

"Let me think." He thought for a while. "Yes. There is one other person who might have known all of them."

Everyone looked at him expectantly.

"The only person I can think of is a General who used to dine with the drivers at the Red stables. General Crispinus was his name. He doesn't come around anymore that I know of, but he used to be there quite frequently. So I know he knew Zephyrus. And I think I remember a time when Pedo was at dinner with them too. As I said, before I became his tout. Pedo used to try and get information by himself. Only then he didn't tell people he was a shoemaker. He passed himself off as a *comes* of a governor."

Severus thanked him and told him he could go.

Glabrio got up to go, but hesitated. Then he looked at everyone there, Severus, Vulso, Crantor and Alexander. "Do any of you want to buy some inside information about the chariot races? I can give you a good deal, less than I charge other clients. And you can make a lot of money betting, you know."

Everyone declined and Glabrio left.

"So now where are we," said Severus to his aides, when Glabrio was gone. "Who are the people who definitely or probably knew all three, Zephyrus, Atalanta and Pedo?"

"There was Glabrio, who just left," replied Alexander. "And probably General Crispinus."

"And Pictor," added Vulso. "The painter definitely knew Atalanta and Zephyrus. He said he didn't recognize the painting of Pedo in his shoe shop, but he might be lying about that. After all, Atalanta was once the courtesan of Pedo and Pictor knew about Crispinus, who she was the courtesan of as well. I wouldn't eliminate Pictor."

"And come to think of it," added Severus. "Atalanta's family knew about Pedo, and they knew that she had been raped, but claim they didn't know who raped her. Maybe they found out it was Zephyrus and are lying to us."

"Don't forget Marilla, Atalanta's slave. She met both Zephyrus and Pedo while Atalanta was painting them."

"But none of them so far seems a likely candidate for a triple murderer, for a nemesis," mused Severus. "Even if they knew all three, what could be a motive to kill all of them?"

"What about Septimius Scapula and Mucius, the former governor of Bithynia and his son-in-law *comes*," added Alexander. "They were on trial with Pedo and since Atalanta was Pedo's courtesan at the time, they probably knew her."

"We have to talk to them, of course," replied Severus. "They might readily have a motive to kill Pedo who certainly knew about whatever other crimes they committed in Bithynia and if he spoke about them to his courtesan, that would make her a danger to them. Did they know Zephyrus as well? We'll have to find out."

"We've located both Scapula and Mucius in the Urbs," spoke up Proculus. "It seems they just returned from vacation in Baiae, at the Crater, where they have been for the past two months. When do you want to see them?"

"The day after tomorrow," replied Severus. "To prepare for them I want to get some information from their prosecutor first, particularly about other crimes they may have committed."

"The day after tomorrow it will be. At the 3rd hour. I'll send messages to both of them right now. But what about tomorrow? What will be on the agenda for tomorrow?"

"Tomorrow, I want to talk to someone who has not been honest with us, who has deliberately lied to us, to put it bluntly. Someone who told us that they didn't know Atalanta knew Pedo?"

"Who is that?" asked Alexander.

"Novatilla. Atalanta's mother. She knew everyone who Atalanta was a courtesan with. So she obviously knew Atalanta had been with Pedo for some years. Yet she told us she never heard of Pedo. That was a lie. So I will see her tomorrow and confront her with her lie. Quintus, send her a message ordering her to come to my chambers at the 3rd hour tomorrow morning."

"I will do that right now."

"Good. We've had a constructive day. And now there's still time to finish our game of *latrunculi*," he said to Alexander. "Bring back the board with our game."

It took some time to finish. Alexander was getting better with each game and he had some winning chances. But Severus saw further and caught him in a swindle, winning the game. It amused both of them, but the winner more than the loser.

SCROLL IV

XVIII

NOVATILLA

Novatilla showed up at Severus' chambers the next morning at the 3rd hour, accompanied by her granddaughter Vipsania. When Novatilla was called in to see the judge, Vulso and Vipsania strolled outside together into the Forum of Augustus. They mingled with the crowd watching criminal trials in progress in the colonnades. They also stopped to admire the beautiful Temple of Mars the Avenger. However, Vulso and Vipsania were more interested in each other than in the trials or the buildings. They arranged another tryst for the next night.

Meanwhile, Severus was ready to confront Novatilla. He waited until he was alone with her, without any of his assistants present.

"Novatilla, I've learned that Atalanta was once the courtesan of the shoemaker Pedo, who was once a wealthy man, a *Comes* of the governor of Bithynia. Why didn't you tell me that when I first mentioned Pedo to you as the third victim?"

"You only asked about a shoemaker named Pedo."

Severus gave her a dubious look. "You don't expect me to believe that you didn't know that the shoemaker Pedo was one and the same person as the *Comes* Pedo?"

"Why not? That could have been the case. Pedo is not an uncommon name."

"But it wasn't the case, was it? Because even if you didn't actually know they were one and the same, the name Pedo would have prompted you to mention a *Comes* named Pedo as someone your daughter had been with. But you didn't do that. So, Novatilla, I want to know why you concealed relevant information from me when we first talked. Why didn't you tell me that the Pedo who had been murdered was or might have been someone your daughter had spent time with as his courtesan?"

Severus accompanied his questions with a hard look at Novatilla. She let her head hang for a few moments and then lifted it up and looked straight back at the judge.

"You're right. I knew that the *Comes* Pedo had become the shoemaker Pedo and I didn't mention it."

"Why not? Didn't you think it was something I should know in the investigation of your daughter's murder?"

"I didn't think it was relevant."

"I don't believe that, Novatilla. You obviously knew it was relevant. So why didn't you tell me?"

"Because I suspected they had both been murdered by the same person and I didn't want my family involved with the murderer. I wanted nothing to do with him."

"Who is this person you believe killed your daughter and Pedo?"

Novatilla took a deep breath. "Pedo was once a *Comes* to the governor of Bithynia, as I'm sure you now know. And my daughter was Pedo's courtesan. He told her plenty about the corruption of the governor Scapula and his viper son-in-law Mucius and what they had done in Bithynia. They robbed that province blind. And maybe Pedo was involved in their crimes, I don't know, but he certainly knew about those two. So I wouldn't be surprised if they killed my daughter and Pedo to silence them. The dead don't bite, as the saying goes. So I believed that if I told you, they would next come after me and then my granddaughter, thinking we also knew about their crimes." She concluded with a confident look.

Severus still didn't believe her and told her so. "It's a facile explanation, Novatilla, but I don't believe it. I want you to tell me the truth."

She set her face in a rigid, defiant look and then got up to leave. "I'll think it over," she said. "That's what I'll do." She stopped at the door. "What are you going to do, Judge?"

"Question Scapula and Mucius."

That night, Severus had a talk with Aulus about his future.

"I hear that you want to transfer from your legion in Cappadocia to a legion fighting the Germans on the Danube."

"Yes, Tata, I want to take part in the war."

"I wish you would reconsider. Your mother, as you know, is fearful. War is dangerous…"

Aulus interrupted. "I know what Mama thinks and I respect her feelings. But I want to do what *I* want to do and that is to take part in the war. And Tata, I am a little surprised at you taking this attitude. Didn't you always want to be in the army?"

"Yes. As you know."

"I don't believe you wanted to be in the army to be a clerk, which is essentially what I am, even though I have the title of Equestrian Tribune."

Severus didn't know what to say. Aulus was right about him.

"Besides, Tata, I have already put my transfer in motion. A Tribune from one of the legions on the Danube is, like me, temporarily assigned to the Castra Peregrina to report on affairs in his area. We've become friends and he says he can and will swing the transfer for me. So the die is cast, as Caesar once said. I'm headed for the northern front."

There was only one thing for Severus to say and he said it. "I'm proud of you, Aulus."

"I know Tata," smiled Aulus. "I'm proud of myself as well."

When Severus recounted the conversation with Aulus to his wife, Artemisia's comment was succinct. "Fools, both of you. Roman men. Fools."

XIX

SCAPULA AND MUCIUS

Before Severus saw Scapula or Mucius, he sent a message to their prosecutor in their trial before the Senate, Tiberius Sosius Tertullus. The message asked Tertullus if there were other crimes or accusations of illegalities brought against the governor of Bithynia besides the *repetundae* extortion he had been on trial for.

Tertullus sent back a large file which he said contained information on numerous other allegations of illegality charged by the provincials against Scapula. Besides the charge of accepting a bribe to acquit a murderer that Scapula had been tried for in the Senate, Scapula was alleged to have regularly accepted bribes to obtain favorable legal decisions, to hand out government jobs and contracts and for favorable treatment in general.

The evidence to back up these accusations was not readily available to the Roman Senate because the witnesses were in Bithynia and only one, the son of the murder victim killed by the wrongfully acquitted murderer, could be found to come to Rome to testify.

Severus and Alexander then turned their attention to the file Tertullus had sent and began reading.

"A disgrace," commented Severus as he read through the file, "a disgrace that these crimes are still going on in our age, under Marcus Aurelius, where good government is the imperial objective. In the days of the Republic, the tradition of exploiting provinces was not uncommon, but now? I know it goes on, but I never realized the extent until reading over these files."

Severus called Vulso and Crantor into his chambers and started reporting the various allegations made against Scapula.

"I want to discuss how to deal with these two criminals, Scapula and Mucius, in light of these allegations. Pedo must have known about some, if not all of them."

"Do any of these also include allegations against Mucius and Pedo?" asked Vulso.

"Most don't mention anyone other than Scapula, but by inference include his *Comites*, although which ones it doesn't say. But here are two that specifically name Mucius and Pedo as accomplices. They are the ones who actually handled the bribe money."

"What were the cases?"

"One concerns a bribe to give someone the contract to build a temple. The bribe was for 500,000 sesterces. Another was a bribe to appoint someone to a job inspecting roads and bridges. Another 500,000 sesterces."

"Of course," commented Vulso. "Becoming an inspector of public works is a way to make money. A corrupt inspector could extort money from whoever constructed a road or bridge, by approving or not approving the construction job. Paying off the inspector guarantees approval. It's an old trick."

"There are also allegations that these crimes are just a part of what they did. Most victims never complained, fearing retaliation. There are allegations that a huge amount of money was extorted from the province and that most of it was secreted somewhere. Only the criminals knew where, though attempts were made to find the money and compensate the provincials."

Severus closed the file. "I think we're ready for Scapula and Mucius now."

The next morning at the 3rd hour, Scapula appeared at the judge's chambers, accompanied by an entourage of four slaves and a lawyer and the lawyer's law clerk.

In the anteroom, court clerk Proculus counted up the six people, learning who was who. "*Clarissime*," Proculus addressed Scapula, "you mentioned you would have nine people with you, including Mucius and his lawyer and slave. But I don't see Mucius or his lawyer or slave. Where are they?"

"I don't know," answered Scapula. "My son-in-law was supposed to meet me here this morning with his lawyer. So I expect he'll be here shortly. We had dinner last night, but he was called away. He received a message tablet and just left, saying he would see me here this morning. He had a big smile on his face when he left, so I suppose everything is all right and he'll be here momentarily."

"I'll tell the judge and he can decide how to proceed right now."

Proculus went into Severus' chambers and told him, Vulso, Flaccus and Alexander that Scapula and his entourage were there, but Mucius was not, relating what had happened the night before at dinner causing Mucius to leave.

Severus and his entourage looked at each other, one after the other. "Are you thinking what I'm thinking?" asked the judge.

Everyone shook their heads up and down.

"What do you want to do?" asked Proculus.

"Bring in Scapula and his lawyers and we'll question him."

"And Mucius?"

"We'll have to wait. Maybe he'll show up."

"I'm sure he'll show up," said Flaccus with a wry smile. "But whether alive or dead is the question."

Proculus went back to the anteroom and escorted Scapula and his lawyer and his lawyer's law clerk into Severus' chambers.

Severus stood up as they entered. He was dressed in his formal judicial toga for the interview. Scapula addressed the judge as *eminentissime* and made a motion as if to head to Severus to exchange greeting kisses between Roman nobility. But Severus, while calling Scapula by his senatorial honorific *clarissime*, sat down without a greeting kiss. This was not entirely an insult, but Scapula could read it as a bad omen, an expression of disfavor on the part of the judge. It was a correct reading.

Scapula introduced his lawyer as Marcus Statilius Habitus. He was a member of the Senatorial Order as was displayed by his dress of a toga over a tunic showing a broad red-purple stripe. Severus acknowledged him with a slight bow of his head as *clarissime*, but did not approach for a greeting kiss. Habitus also took that as a sign of the judge's displeasure, not so much for him, but for his client.

Severus looked over the three people now seated across the table from him. Scapula and his lawyer were both corpulent. The law clerk was thin. Scapula had no hair, Habitus some hair, and the law clerk a full head of hair. Each wore a short beard in the style of the Emperor.

"What is this all about?" asked Scapula, his voice strong, but not quite hostile.

"Your former *Comes*, Pedo, has been murdered."

"Is that so? I didn't know that. But I can't say I'm sorry. He was convicted by the Senate of extorting money from the province of Bithynia, which I governed as Propraetor. He betrayed me. As the Senate found, I was entirely innocent. He was guilty."

"Did you know his courtesan, Atalanta?"

"Yes. A very beautiful woman and very accomplished on the lyre, as I remember. After returning from Bithynia, we would occasionally have dinner, that is, me, my son-in-law and Pedo, and his courtesan would sometimes play for us."

"She has been murdered too."

Scapula didn't bat an eye. "I didn't know that either. When did this all happen?"

"About a month ago."

"That explains it. We were on vacation on the Bay of Neapolis for the last two months, at Baiae specifi-cally." Severus, of course, knew Baiae was a favored vacation land for the rich, famous for its gambling, its wild parties and its debauchery. Severus had been there to investigate the murder of General Cyclops some years before. Otherwise, while liking other parts of the Bay of Neapolis for a vacation, he avoided Baiae.

"Did you know a charioteer from the Red faction named Zephyrus?"

Before Scapula had a chance to answer, Proculus came in with a message tablet for the judge. "A member of the *Vigiles* just brought it."

Severus read it, his face becoming rigid. "There's been another murder. He was found in an alley on the Aventine Hill, his throat cut, and the number IV written on his cheek in blood."

Severus looked at Scapula. "You know who it is, don't you?"

"Me? How should I know?"

"He was lured to his death the same way Zephyrus, Pedo and Atalanta were lured to their deaths?"

"I don't know anything about that. As I just told you, the family, and that includes my daughter and Mucius, have been out of Rome on vacation for two months. I know nothing about those murders or how they were perpetrated."

Severus gave him a searching look, but couldn't tell whether he was lying or not.

"From what I know, it must be your son-in-law, Mucius, who has been murdered."

"Mucius murdered? You're just guessing. I don't believe it." He looked doubtful, though a hint of fear crossed his face. He looked at Proculus. "Get me some water, will you?"

Proculus went out and came back with a glass of water. Scapula drank it up and composed himself. He said to Severus. "Mucius murdered? I'll believe it when I see it."

Severus shrugged and continued his questioning. "What can you tell me about the tablet he received last night and who sent it? Did he say anything before he left?"

"Nothing. He just got up and left, as far as I know. Maybe someone else at dinner might remember something. I don't."

Proculus interrupted and spoke to the judge. "There's an officer of the *Vigiles* here, the one who brought the tablet. He has a *cisium* chariot with a seat waiting to take you to the crime scene. He said all the *Vigiles* had been alerted a month ago by the Prefect of the City that if there were any murder with a number written in blood on the victim's cheek, they were to report it to you immediately. And so they have."

Severus got up. "Vulso, get Straton and Crantor and we'll all go to the murder scene. Alexander, you come too. I'll go in the chariot. You and the others can come by foot, although you'll probably get there ahead of me, given Rome's traffic congestion at this time of day."

The judge turned to Scapula and his lawyers.

"I need you or someone here with you to come and identify the body."

Scapula shook his head, "I'm not going. You can take one of my slaves waiting for me in your anteroom. They all know Mucius."

"You can go home then. Ask around if anyone remembers anything connected with Mucius leaving the dinner last night. Anything he said. Find out who delivered the message. But I'm coming to your house after I leave the crime scene. Have everyone who was at dinner last night waiting for me. I want to question them and also I haven't finished questioning you. We will continue at your house in a few hours. Right now, though, I'm going to the crime scene and see what I can learn there."

Severus bolted out. Proculus stayed and made sure to notice the expression on the face of Scapula. It was grim, but otherwise unreadable.

XX

A CRIME SCENE

As he predicted, when Severus arrived at the murder scene by chariot, Vulso, Straton, Alexander, Crantor and one of Scapula's slaves were already there. Even though wheeled vehicles were banned from Rome during the daytime, except for government chariots like the one that brought Severus, pedestrian traffic was still dense and chaotic, making moving about the City difficult. At least, thought Severus, on a hot summery day like today, the chariot's movement provided some breeze, though the unpleasant and smelly *aer infamis* of the huge city could not be avoided.

When Severus got down from the chariot, he was introduced to the centurion of the *Vigiles* who was in charge of the crime scene. From the head of the alley where he stood, Severus could see that halfway down the alley there was a body lying on the ground.

"We knew to send for you, *eminentissime*, if any body was found with a number written on his cheek.

And here is one we found this morning." He led Severus and those with him down the alley.

The scene was gruesome. A man lay there rigid in death, his eyes open and staring blankly, his throat cut and his head dangling from his neck. There was dried blood on his neck and upper body. The number IV was written in blood on his cheek. Severus turned to Scapula's slave who Vulso had brought with him.

"What's your name?"

"Musa, *eminentissime*."

"Musa, you know Quintus Mucius, is that right?"

"Yes, *eminentissime*. I have seen him many times and know him well."

"Take a look at that body and tell me if you recognize him."

Musa walked to stand over the body and looked at the head. He grimaced and almost threw up, but collected himself."

"It's Quintus Mucius. No doubt about it." A little smile came to his face.

"Were you at the dinner last night when he received a message tablet?"

"Not really, *eminentissime*. I was cleaning the toilet in the kitchen, but I could see into the *triclinium*."

"Do you know who was at the dinner?"

"Yes. I do. It was my master Scapula, his wife Perpetua, his daughter Septimia, and her husband, Mucius. Also. Scapula's business manager and freedman, Myron and his wife Philippa. Those six."

"Did you see when Mucius left?"

"No. I was cleaning the toilet. One moment Mucius was at dinner. The next moment he was gone. That's all I know."

"Thank you, Musa." Severus turned to the centurion. "Is there anything you can tell me about what happened. Did you find anyone who saw something or knows something? Did you find a message tablet on him, for instance?"

"No. The body was found this morning when one of the slaves of that house over there came out to fetch water from the fountain in the plaza at the end of the alley. She said she almost tripped over the body. She screamed, she said, and then called for help. Her mistress came out and then sent her to our *Vigiles* station a few streets away. The *Vigil* who came back with her and saw the body also saw the number IV written on his cheek and came back and told us. We then secured the crime scene and sent for a doctor to examine the body. He said it looked like the victim had been taken from behind. Apparently, he was seized by the hair, his head jerked back and his throat cut with a dagger. Then a *Vigil* was sent to inform you what happened, as we had been instructed to do last month."

"Thank you, centurion, and good work. I'm going to the house of his father-in-law Scapula and will inform the wife and the father-in-law what happened. I want to see for myself how they react to the news. You can take the body away, but hold on to it until you receive instructions from the family, who will want to take the body for cremation or burial.

"And by the way, centurion, would you happen to know the *Vigil* or *Vigiles* who found the bodies of the chariot driver Zephyrus and the woman Atalanta about a month ago?"

"It wasn't me. I'm not sure who it was, but I can easily find out for you."

"Please do so, and have that officer or officers came to my chambers tomorrow morning at the 3rd hour."

"I will do that."

"Thank you again," and with that Severus and those with him headed for the house of Scapula to resume his questioning, both of Scapula, and of the diners the night before.

XXI

THE DOMUS OF SCAPULA

When Severus reached the *domus* of Scapula, all the diners from the night before were waiting in the *tablinum* office, behind the atrium, seated around a table. There was Scapula, his wife Perpetua, his daughter Septimia, and Scapula's business manager and freedman, Myron and his wife Philippa. Only Mucius was missing from the diners. Severus noticed that all the family were on the heavy side, though all Scapula's slaves he had seen were quite thin.

The table was set with wine and fruit already waiting. The wine was served in expensive transparent see-through glasses and the fruit, grapes and dates, were in a gold bowl. Severus, Alexander, Vulso, Straton and Crantor sat down opposite the family and everyone proceeded to have some wine and fruit. Scapula introduced everyone present to the judge.

"It's my sad duty to inform you," began Severus, "that Quintus Mucius has been murdered."

"You told us that in your chambers," said Scapula, matter of factly, "or at least implied as much. So we are not surprised by what you're confirming now."

But surprised or not, Severus noticed, no one seemed to be grieving or even looked upset in any way. That included Mucius' wife. Everyone appeared normal, as if nothing had happened. Somehow Severus didn't think they were all Stoic philosophers.

"I want to know what happened last night. I understand Mucius received a message and left. Who delivered the message?"

"My *ianitor*," replied Scapula, "says that a young boy he never saw before came to the door with a Vitellian tablet and said it was for Quintus Mucius. He handed the tablet to my doorman and left in a hurry. The *ianitor* came into the *triclinium* and handed the tablet to Mucius. Mucius opened it, read it, and his eyes widened and a smile crossed his face. He then got up, told us he had to leave on a business matter, and left. That's all."

"Septimia, you're his wife. Didn't you ask him where he was going? Didn't he tell you?"

Septimia was a rigid woman. She sat stiff and upright in her chair. Her face was set. Her glare icy. "No. He didn't tell me anything. He never told me where he was going, and I never told him where I went either." She didn't say 'good riddance', but her manner and look implied it.

"Do any of you know of any enemies he had? Anyone who might have killed him?

There was a titter of smothered laughter. Septimia came straight to the point. "Anyone who met him would like to kill him. He was arrogant, a tyrant, a viper, a thoroughly unpleasant person." She glared at her father. "I will never understand why anyone would choose him for an arranged marriage with his daughter. But, of course, I was only 14 at the time and didn't know any better."

Scapula didn't react at all. He had undoubtedly heard this many times.

"Does anyone have anything to add?"

No one did.

"Then, I'd like to continue my talk with Scapula and so I would ask everyone else to leave, so I can talk to him alone."

Everyone got up and ambled back toward the atrium.

"Tell my lawyer and his assistant to come here," said Scapula to his wife. When they had all left, Habitus and his young assistant came into the *tablinum* and took chairs on either side of Scapula.

"What do you want to know?" said Scapula, somewhat testily. "I'm busy, so make it fast." He omitted Severus' honorific and his tone of voice had a challenge in it.

Severus always loved a challenge and hurled back an answer. "Senator, I am a *iudex selectus*, a Special Judge charged by Prefect of the City to solve now four murders. I will take as much time as I need. How busy you are is irrelevant. I am interviewing you here in your home, but if you'd prefer, I can convene an official court and question you from the Tribunal instead. Is that what you want?"

Scapula didn't answer. His lawyer Habitus did, however, and politely tried to smooth things over.

"*Eminentissime,* my client wants to help you any way he can in your investigations, as do I. So please feel free to ask any question you like and take as much time as you feel necessary."

Severus nodded to the lawyer and then addressed Scapula. "If Mucius was such a hateful person, why did you marry your daughter to him? Why did you make him one of your *Comites*?"

"He may have been an unpleasant person, but he was a capable assistant for me as one of my *Comes*. And as for marrying my daughter, I did not know his character at the time of the marriage arrangement. He came from a noble family and seemed a good match. That's all."

Severus shook his head in disbelief at the negligence and lack of concern this father had for his daughter. But then, Severus knew Scapula was a corrupt person, that he had extorted money from the province he governed, had accepted bribes to deliver unjust verdicts and had handed out jobs and contracts for money. So why was it so surprising that he would have a viper like Mucius as his assistant and marry him to his daughter?

Severus changed the subject. "When we left off in my chambers, I had asked you whether you knew the charioteer for the Reds, Zephyrus. I repeat that question. Did you know him?"

"No. I don't associate with chariot drivers, of any faction."

The questioning continued for almost an hour, with Severus probing Scapula and his crimes as governor, his relationship to Pedo, his knowledge of

Atalanta, and the role of Mucius in his affairs. But Scapula admitted nothing, denied everything, and wouldn't give an inch.

In frustration, Severus started to get up to leave but Scapula held up his hand signaling him to wait and asked his lawyer and lawyer's aide to leave. "I want to say something to the judge alone."

When they left, Scapula took a deep breath and said, "Judge, it looks like you've decided to persecute me for crimes people said I committed in Bithynia and anything else you can dredge up. All these accusations are false, I assure you. I am completely innocent of everything." Severus gave him a doubtful look but waited for what it was Scapula really wanted to say. "Therefore, judge, you will understand that I wish to avoid any investigation that will consume my time and my attention and will harass me to no purpose because, as I said, I am totally innocent. Therefore, if you will conclude your business with me quickly, even as of now, and conclude I am innocent of all charges and there is no reason to investigate me further, then I can assure you that it will benefit you as well as me. And I promise your benefit will be substantial, enough, say, to qualify for the Senatorial Order."

Scapula paused. Qualification for the Senatorial Order, Severus well knew, was a million sesterces.

Severus stood up and looked Scapula in the eye. "I don't take bribes," he replied harshly and walked out.

Outside, Vulso was waiting for him with the slave Musa.

"He has something to tell you, judge," advised Vulso. "But he insists it has to be strictly secret."

Severus and Vulso took Musa around a corner, out of sight of Scapula's *domus*.

"What is it, Musa? What do you want to tell me?"

"Just this. I happened to overhear one thing when you were questioning the master. I heard him say he didn't know Zephyrus, the charioteer for the Reds. *Eminentissime*, I know I can't testify against my master in court, but this isn't court, so I can tell you that what he told you was a blatant lie. Zephyrus had dinner here with the senator more than once. And Mucius was present as well. I happen to know that they were trying to bribe Zephyrus to fix races. And it wasn't only Zephyrus. I know for a fact that they also met with charioteers from the Greens and Blues trying to get them to fix races as well. But I don't think any of them agreed to do it. I think Scapula and Mucius eventually had to drop the attempt as a bad idea. But his denial to you, *eminentissime*, was entirely false."

"Thank you, Musa. That's very helpful. I won't tell anyone, of course. And now that we're talking confidentially, tell me about Scapula's household."

"There are 27 slaves, including me. Scapula is very strict with us. We get slapped for the slightest mistake, sometimes whipped as well. His wife Perpetua is also that way with the female slaves. There's an overseer of the household slaves who is very big and very strong. A former gladiator, a Gaul, named Adebugius. Everyone is afraid of him. Also, you may have noticed that all the slaves are thin, though the master and his family are fat. That's because the slaves are not fed enough. Sometimes we get food treats to keep us in line, but usually food is scarce for us, deliberately."

"Thank you, Musa. I appreciate your help. If you hear or know anything else relevant, please let me know. Your help will not go unrewarded."

Musa looked at the judge expectantly, waiting to hear what the reward might, what he was hoping it might be. Severus understood. "You know, Musa, the court of the Urban Prefect sometimes buys slaves who have been helpful and useful to it. Sometimes the court buys them and frees them if they are very helpful."

That was what Musa wanted to hear. "I will try to be very helpful, *eminentissime*."

"You are a slave. Can you get away from the house without much trouble?"

"I can manage it. Why?"

"If you want to contact me or tell me of any developments, you can leave a message for me at the bookstore of Caelius on the Vicus Sandalarius. Caelius will get it to me. We can also use the bookstore stacks for secret meetings if you need to talk to us. Caelius will arrange it."

When Musa left, Vulso made a comment. "We now have a spy inside Scapula's house."

"Even more. We now know that Scapula had a reason to kill all four of the victims. Each knew about one or more of his crimes. He had reason to silence each of them. The dead don't bite."

"We also know," continued Vulso, "if Scapula ordered the murders, who he could have used to carry them out. His Gallic ex-gladiator Adebugius, is a good possibility."

"That's right, Vulso. Scapula and Adebugius are now our prime suspects."

Late that afternoon, with everyone assembled in Severus' chambers, they discussed the day's events and Severus told them all about Scapula's attempt to bribe him with a million sesterces.

"Can you imagine the hubris of that man? Trying to bribe a Roman judge, a *iudex selectus*."

"He probably thinks everyone is as corrupt as he is," commented Vulso.

"He may not be that far off," commented Flaccus cynically.

"Wasn't that Cicero's opinion when he remarked that Rome was not Plato's Republic, but Romulus' shit pile?"

"I can't think of Rome as a shit pile under Marcus Aurelius," countered Severus. "Even though he warns us we cannot realistically expect Plato's Republic from his reign, he is already one of our greatest Emperors. He has been Emperor now for 12 years, and before that Caesar to Antoninus Pius for 21 years. He's not only an extremely experienced ruler, but a virtuous, philosophical person. However, I have to admit that his reign, through no fault of his own, has been punctuated by disasters. First, a Tiber flood inundated large areas of the City. Then there was a major war with Persia. Then a devastating plague ravaged Rome and still ravages parts of the Empire. Then there was the untimely death of his co-Emperor Lucius Verus, and now there's another major war, this time with German barbarians."

"It shows," commented Flaccus, "that even great rulers are at the mercy of outside events."

"What it shows is that the Stoic philosopher Epictetus is right," replied Severus ruefully. "We can control only our own power to choose and refuse, our own desires and aversions, our own opinions, all internal to our minds. External events and things are not under our control. Not our possessions, not the opinions of others, not even our bodies. No wonder Marcus Aurelius, even though an Emperor, finds Epictetus, a former slave, his most influential philosopher."

"Yes," replied Flaccus, "Marcus Aurelius may cultivate and even elevate the virtues of our civilization, but Scapula cultivates and elevates the shit pile.

XXII

JUDGE SEVERUS IS ARRESTED FOR MURDER

That night, around midnight, Scorpus, the slave in charge of the household, came into the master bedroom and shook the judge lightly, until he woke up.

"*Domine*," he said quietly so as not to wake up Artemisia, "there are four members of the *Vigiles* at the door, a centurion among them. They ask to see you. They say it's urgent."

"I hope nothing bad has happened," said Severus getting up from bed and straightening out his tunic. He followed Scorpus to the front door of the apartment.

There was a centurion just inside the door, with four other soldiers behind him.

"Are you Marcus Flavius Severus?"

"Yes. What is it?"

The centurion stepped forward. "You're under arrest. Please come with us."

Severus stepped back, with a surprised look. "What? You must be joking. What am I being arrested for?"

"You are under arrest for murder."

"Nonsense. Who am I supposed to have murdered?"

"As the murderer, you should know," replied the centurion gruffly. "Now, no more questions. We have the evidence. Come with us to our station. Cohort VII of the *Vigiles*. It's on the Caelian Hill, not far away. Come voluntarily or we will take you by force."

"This is a ridiculous mistake. However, I will come with you now and straighten things out. First, I must change out of my bed clothes."

"We will wait."

Severus went back inside and told Artemisia what was happening.

"This is absurd."

"Yes. But I have to go with them. This can't be treated lightly. Mistakes can lead to other mistakes. I have to set things right as fast as possible. Scorpus, is Aulus in his room?"

"No, *domine*. He went to a party of some sort and is not yet back."

"Then I need our slaves to get help. Wake up Tryphon, Glykon and Sarapion."

Scorpus rushed through the house from room to room, calling the slaves to wake up and come to Severus' bedroom. Once there, Severus quickly issued orders. "Scorpus, I want you to go immediately to the home of the Urban Prefect and tell him there's been some sort of mistake and I've been arrested for murder and taken to the station of Cohort VII of the *Vigiles* on the Caelian Hill. Tryphon, I want you to go to the apartment of my assessor Flaccus and tell him what's happened. Sarapion, I want you to find Vulso. I want both Flaccus and Vulso to come immediately to the *Vigiles* station. Tell them that I don't know who I'm supposed to have murdered, the *Vigiles* won't tell me and I don't know why they think I'm their culprit.

"Glykon, I want you to come with me and stay by my side. I don't entirely trust the *Vigiles*, nor to be alone in their hands. I want you to witness whatever happens. Artemisia, when Aulus returns home, let him know what's going on. Ask him to find Straton and Crantor, and bring them and himself to the *Vigiles* station."

Severus then changed into a formal toga over a tunic with the narrow red-purple stripes of his Equestrian Order. He kissed Artemisia and, with Glycon in tow, left with the *Vigiles*.

XXIII

SEVERUS IN PRISON

It was the middle of the night and one of the *Vigiles* led the way through the streets to the station of Cohort VII with a torch. On the way, Severus once again asked the centurion who had been murdered and what made them think he, a judge, had anything to do with it. He also asked the centurion his name. The centurion did not reply to any of his questions.

"I've notified the Urban Prefect," Severus told him. "He'll want to know what this is all about. And he'll want to know why you refuse to tell me the crime you think I committed and the evidence for it."

That made the centurion speak up. "I only answer to the Prefect of the *Vigiles*, not the Prefect of the City."

"You'll find that the Prefect of the *Vigiles* answers to the Prefect of the City, so I hope your attitude is only a temporary expression of some sort of turf rivalry between police forces. Because if it is not, you will personally suffer the consequences."

"Shut up, murderer. You're the one who is about to suffer consequences."

Severus kept quiet as they made their way down the Caelian Hill. But two basic questions rattled around in his mind. Who had been murdered? Why did the *Vigiles* think he was a murderer? A third thought added to his disturbance. Who was this centurion and why was he so hostile? In any event, he would soon find out.

After a brief walk, they reached their destination, the *excubitorium* of Cohort VII of the *Vigiles*.

There were nine cohorts of the *Vigiles*. Each had an *excubitorium* for 1,000 troops whose job it was to fight fires and patrol the City, especially at night. The nine stations were scattered throughout the 14 regions of the City.

Severus was escorted into the main entrance and motioned to stand before a *Vigil* seated behind a desk. The space was crowded with *Vigiles* and clerks and prisoners going to and fro. The *Vigiles* were the night watch, after all, and this time of night was their busy time.

"He's under arrest for murder," said the centurion to the desk officer. "Put him in a jail cell to await trial."

"I'm a judge in the Court of the Urban Prefect and a *iudex selectus*, appointed by the Urban Prefect. I have a *cognitio* to solve a series of murders," said Severus to the desk officer. "I demand to be brought before a judge so that I can ask for *vadimonium*, for bail. Also, members of my staff will be arriving shortly. They are a Tribune in the legion XII Fulminata, a centurion in the Urban Cohort and my assessor and lawyer. There also may be a few others. I expect each one to be admitted into my presence, so that I can confer with them in private.

"I am totally innocent of murder and this arrest is a farce or a contrived attack on the court of the Urban Prefect by criminals seeking to avoid justice. The fact that your centurion has been duped, does not mean that you have to be duped as well. Be forewarned that any mistreatment of me will carry the most severe repercussions."

The desk officer did not reply, but neither Severus' confident speech nor his Equestrian striped tunic escaped notice. The desk clerk motioned to a *Vigil* standing nearby. "You will be treated according to your rank," said the desk officer to Severus, and with that, Severus and Glycon were led by the *Vigil* with a bunch of keys hanging from his belt down a corridor of jail cells. One after another was crowded with riff-raff, drunks, petty thieves, and *grassatores* – street thugs. Most were sleeping on hay beds on the floor or standing around yacking or arguing. In this jail, bread and water were supplied by the jailors, but other food and drink and supplies had to be brought by family members. There were buckets in the cells for excrement. The loud noises, putrid smells and general feelings of ill health and disgust penetrated easily into the corridor.

These jail cells were only for the purposes of holding defendants for trial or for execution of sentence. No one was ever sentenced to prison under Roman law. Beatings, exile and death were the basic punishments, often along with confiscation of property and loss of status.

They reached a jail cell that was unoccupied. "You're lucky," laughed the jailor, opening the cell door, "that we don't put you in one of the cells below ground, where you could enjoy the filth and smell in total darkness."

"You're lucky," rejoined Severus, "that you don't put me there because treatment like that of a Roman judge and Equestrian will eventually be punished."

With that, Severus and Glykon were led into the cell. It was small, but unoccupied. They both plopped down onto beds of hay on the floor.

"Let's go to sleep," said Severus to Glykon, "We can await developments in the land of Morpheus."

About an hour later, developments started to happen. The first to arrive was Aulus, dressed in full military uniform of a legionary Tribune.

He was escorted to the cell where Severus and Glykon were fast asleep. "Tata, wake up. It's me," said Aulus shaking his father. Severus blinked and shook off sleep.

"Aulus. I'm glad you're here. Have you found out anything?"

"No, Tata. Mama told me you had been arrested and had been taken here about an hour before. I quickly put on my uniform, and went to find Straton. I woke him up and told him what happened. He's going to get Crantor. I then came straight here. When I got here, I asked the desk officer what's going on. I said to him that the idea that you murdered anyone was ridiculous. I said this situation was of interest to the military, so I wanted to know why you were arrested. But he wouldn't tell me anything. 'We don't answer to the military', he told me."

A half an hour later Vulso arrived. He also recounted his attempt to find out what was happening, why Severus had been arrested, who had been killed. "I told the *Vigiles* out front that the Urban Prefect and the Urban Cohort wanted to know. But however loudly I yelled at them, however much pressure I put on, I was told 'the *Vigiles* don't answer to the Urban Cohort.'" He shrugged. "Rivalry between police forces. It's a real pain."

A half hour later Flaccus arrived. The judge's assessor, and now an experienced lawyer in his own right, came down the corridor smiling.

"I never thought I'd find you in a jail cell, judge."

"I never thought I would be here," replied Severus. "And I don't even know why I'm here."

"I do," answered Flaccus. "I know why you're here, who you're supposed to have murdered and what the so-called evidence is that led to your arrest."

Severus, Aulus and Vulso looked at him with expressions of wonder. "How did you find out these things?" asked Severus. "We all tried to find out but were met with obstinance. None of our arguments seemed to carry any weight with them. They said only that they don't answer to anyone, the army, the Urban Cohort, anyone. How did you find out?"

"You used the wrong argument," replied Flaccus laughing. "I used an argument that was irresistible."

"What was that?" asked Aulus.

"Money. I know that generally their practice is to hold onto information and I know what loosens their tongues. So I came here prepared. Then I sought out a *Vigil* I knew and bribed him. He was happy to find out and tell me whatever I wanted to know. So while the *Vigiles* may not answer to the army or to the Urban Cohort, they have no trouble in spilling everything to a pouch of silver coins."

Everyone laughed. "Find yourself a seat of hay," said Severus, "and tell us everything."

They all sat down in the hay and Flaccus began. "First thing you have to know is who was murdered. Get ahold of yourself now. The person murdered last night was Septimius Scapula."

"What? Our primary suspect?"

"Yes. Your primary suspect. I would take him off the suspect list now. He was murdered in the park on the Caelian Hill near your *insula*, judge. Where you regularly walk your dog."

"What was he doing there?"

"According to Scapula's wife, Perpetua, earlier last evening he received a message tablet from you, judge."

"From me? I never sent him any message. It's clearly a forgery. What did it say?"

"Scapula's wife told the *Vigiles* when they came to report his murder, that her husband received a tablet saying that the writer had changed his mind and was interested in the Senatorial amount. Perpetua said Scapula was delighted and told her he was right, that anyone could be bribed. He then told her he had offered you a million sesterces to drop your investigation of him. He said you refused at first, but now, now you changed your mind and sent this message tablet.

"Perpetua said also that the message told Scapula to go alone to the park across from your *insula* and you would meet him on the bench furthest from the entrance to the park, a bench mostly secluded by trees. Scapula read to Perpetua from the tablet that you would meet him at the 5th night hour.

"He then took his bodyguard, the ex-gladiator Adebugius, and they went to the park. He left Adebugius outside the park and went in to meet you. Adebugius waited for him to return, and waited and waited. Finally, he became nervous and went into the park and found Scapula dead, sprawled at the foot of the bench, his throat slit from ear to ear. He then went back to the street, found a passer-by and told him to get the *Vigiles*, which he did. The *Vigiles* dealt with the body and went with Adebugius to inform Perpetua what had happened. She told them about the message. The *Vigiles* then went to your *insula* to arrest you for murdering Scapula."

"So the false message tablet was sent to lure Scapula to his death, just like the other message tablets lured the chariot driver, Atalanta, Pedo and Mucius to their deaths. Was any number written on Scapula's cheek?"

"Yes. The number 'V' was written in blood. He was the 5th victim."

There was a commotion in the corridor. The jailor with keys opened the door and a centurion of the *Vigiles*, not the one who arrested Severus, came in and was very polite. "*Eminentissime*, the Urban Prefect himself has come with a Tribunal and will hold court down the hall now. He is prepared to immediately grant you bail."

Severus, Flaccus, Aulus, Vulso and Glykon were led out of the cell and down the hall and into an empty room. In front, there was a Tribunal set up along with a statue of Jupiter Fidius, the god of good faith, whose presence made the room into an official courtroom. The Urban Prefect, Lucius Sergius Paullus, was personally seated on the Tribunal, a big smile on his face followed by a sleepy yawn. Severus walked up to the Tribunal and stood in front of it.

"Court is now open," said the Prefect. "Is a motion for bail being made?"

"It is, *clarissime*. I make a motion for *vadimonium*."

"Granted. *Vadimonium* is set at 1 sesterce. Court is now closed."

The Prefect got down from the Tribunal and exchanged greeting kisses with Severus. "Now we can all go home and go to sleep. I'll talk to you tomorrow, judge."

They all then went home and went to sleep.

SCROLL V

XXIV

DEDUCING A CRIME

It was late the next morning when everyone gathered in Judge Severus' chambers in the Forum of Augustus.

"I didn't get all that much sleep at first," began Severus. "What was on my mind was the question, who sent the false message tablet to Scapula? It had to be someone who knew that Scapula had attempted to bribe me to the tune of one million sesterces. Who was that person?

"It was either someone Scapula himself told about the bribe attempt or someone who heard about it from a different source, namely me."

"Let's first consider Scapula. He didn't tell his wife anything about it until he received the message tablet. Who else would he have told? I can't think of anyone. And why would he tell anyone that he tried to bribe a judge? And failed in the attempt? Does anyone have a suggestion?"

No one did.

"So if Scapula didn't tell anyone, and the only people I told about it are in this room, I have to ask. Did any of you mention it to anyone else?"

All shook their heads in negative gestures, except Alexander and Vulso.

"I told my wife, Persephone," said Alexander. "But I'm sure she didn't tell anyone else."

Vulso followed. "I have to admit that I did tell someone, but someone with no connection to Scapula."

"Who did you tell?"

"I told Vipsania."

"You mean Atalanta's daughter? That Vipsania?"

"Yes. Her. We had a tryst the other night and it was just pillow talk. But she's not connected to Scapula, nor is anyone in her family. Atalanta's mother, Novatilla, Atalanta's bodyguard Heron, none of them would have any reason to send a false message to Scapula, let alone to kill him."

Severus mulled it over. "Vulso, I have to say I'm surprised at your carelessness here. It's not like you."

"I'm sorry, judge. You're right. I shouldn't have told Vipsania anything. I just wasn't thinking with the upper part of my body."

"Vipsania may not be connected directly to Scapula," said Severus, "but her mother Atalanta was in the sense that Scapula was the main defendant in the trial of the person Atalanta was living with at the time. Her lover Pedo."

"But Pedo is dead," countered Vulso. "Atalanta is dead. So even if Vipsania told her family about the attempted bribe, what could be this family's motivation to do anything to Scapula, let alone kill him?"

"We have to figure this out. Someone who knew about the failed bribe attempt used it to lure Scapula to a place where he could be killed? That's certain. So there has to be an answer," said Severus, as much to himself as to the people in the room. "There has to be one."

Severus rose, clasped his hands behind his back and started to pace the room. Back and forth, back and forth. No one said anything. Everyone knew not to disturb him when he went into one of his deep meditations. After about a quarter of an hour, Severus stopped, with a look of awareness in his eyes, a small smile on his face.

"I have a theory that explains everything. The only problem is that it may be impossible."

"That seems like a major impediment," said Flaccus. "You had better tell us anyway."

"All right. I will." Severus sat down and took a gulp of wine.

"Who had the strongest reason to kill Zephyrus, the Red charioteer?"

"Scapula's reason, to silence him about a bribe attempt, was a reason," answered Alexander. "But I don't know how strong it was. Not very, I suppose, since Zephyrus hadn't reported it and probably wouldn't."

"And also," pointed out Crantor, "Scapula tried the same thing on drivers of the Blues, Greens and Whites, and none of them has been murdered."

"Anyone else have a motive to kill Zephyrus?" asked Severus.

"Atalanta had the best reason," said Artemisia. "Zephyrus raped her. She may have wanted to kill him for revenge, or justice. But she is dead, of course."

"Who had the strongest motive to kill Scapula and Mucius?"

"Probably Pedo," suggested Vulso. "But he is dead."

"Now we're on the right track," said Severus. Atalanta had a strong motive to kill Zephyrus and Pedo had a strong motive to kill both Mucius and Scapula. They could be the nemises of those three victims. Revenge, or perhaps justice in their minds, could have motivated them. And possibly Pedo might know where extorted money is stashed."

"But they are dead," said Flaccus. "Is that the impossibility you were referring to?"

"Yes. They are dead." Severus paused. "But are they?"

Severus stopped and looked at everyone in turn. They returned blank looks.

"What are you saying?" asked Flaccus. "Are you saying they are not dead?"

"No one identified Pedo as the dead person in his room. He was identified because of where he was found and by the military *signaculum* he was wearing around his neck. Suppose it wasn't Pedo. Suppose it was someone else. Suppose someone put the *signaculum* on a body to create an identification?"

"It did seem strange," commented Vulso, "that he would be wearing his military identification in his home.

People might wear *signacula* when away from home, when traveling in a different city, but in one's own bedroom?"

"But Atalanta was identified by her family as the murdered woman found by the *Vigiles*. The one with the number II written in blood on her face," objected Straton. "What about that?"

"Suppose the family is in on this," shot back Severus. "I've been suspicious of Novatilla because she held back from telling me that Atalanta was Pedo's courtesan, when I first asked whether she knew about someone named Pedo. The explanation she later gave me for holding out didn't convince me. Suppose then that her family knew that it was not Atalanta who was dead, but another woman, and were covering it up. Suppose they know Atalanta is actually alive and hiding somewhere in Rome with Pedo."

"I see," said Vulso. "Then Vipsania could have told them about Scapula's attempt to bribe you. If they are alive, and are the ones together committing murders, then they could have used that information to get at Scapula, to lure him into the park where he could be killed."

"That would also explain the numbers written on the cheeks of all the victims," added Severus. "The numbers were to show that both Atalanta and Pedo were murder victims along with Zephyrus, Mucius and Scapula. It would throw off investigators, as it threw us off. The real victims were Zephyrus, Mucius and Scapula. Pedo would be a natural suspect for killing Scapula and Mucius. Atalanta would be a natural suspect for Zephyrus' death. But being 'dead' removes both of them from any list of suspects.

"So, then, if my theory is correct, Pedo killed all of them, with Atalanta as his accomplice. Remember Pedo was described as big and strong, Scapula's intimidator in Bithynia.

"Also, it could explain who sent the Vitellian message tablets to Zephyrus and Mucius. I wager the tablet to Zephyrus, a Catullus love poem, purported to be an invitation to him from Atalanta for more sex. And possibly the same invitation was in the message to Mucius, who knew Atalanta as Pedo's courtesan and may have lusted after her, and Atalanta knew it. The ruse could still work with Mucius, as it did with Zephyrus, because Mucius and Scapula had been out of Rome, away on vacation for two months and didn't know that Atalanta was supposed to be dead."

"But if Pedo and Atalanta are alive, who are the dead bodies cremated as them?" asked Alexander. "Did they kill two innocent people, a man for Pedo and a woman for Atalanta?"

"I wouldn't do it that way," interjected Proculus. They all turned to him. "Dead bodies are found abandoned in the streets of Rome all the time. If fact, the City Aedile has contracts with undertakers who are paid to collect and dispose of unidentified bodies. We've all probably seen their red clad workers hauling bodies away with hooks to be dumped outside the *pomerium* city limits. There's even a central headquarters on the Esquiline Hill for the organization that deals with unclaimed dead bodies. If I wanted a dead body, I would go to one of the contract undertakers, who are located outside the Esquiline gate and claim to be looking for a missing relative. Maybe a sister for

Atalanta. Someone who looked like her or could pass for her as a dead body. The same for Pedo. Someone who looked similar to him. That's how I would do it."

"That must be the right explanation," replied Severus, "Atalanta and Pedo could have retrieved two bodies, first one at one undertaker, then another the next day from another undertaker. Pedo's body could have been taken by litter to his *insula* at night when the doorman was not on duty. Atalanta's 'body' could have been taken to the alley where it was found. The throats of the bodies would then have been slit and numbers written on their cheeks in their blood, if there was any not dried up, or in the blood of Atalanta and Pedo themselves.

"It's an interesting theory," said Straton. "If you're right, it explains everything. But how do we prove it? Maybe make the rounds of undertakers, showing them the paintings of Atalanta and Pedo that we have. Maybe someone will remember them."

"The only real way to prove your theory, judge," responded Flaccus, "is to find Atalanta and Pedo alive."

"Precisely. And we can start with Vipsania. In my theory, she knows where Atalanta and Pedo are hiding out because she was the person who told them about Scapula's attempt to bribe me. So we have to get her to lead us to them."

"How can we do that?" asked Alexander.

"We have to give Vipsania some information she's certain to pass on to Atalanta and Pedo and have her followed when she goes to where they're hiding out. Vulso, do you have another tryst set up with Vipsania?"

"Yes. Tonight, as a matter of fact. We have our trysts at the Athena's Mantle hotel near *Vicus Piscinae Publicae*, Public Swimming Pool Street. We'll spend the night together. Then in the morning when she leaves the hotel, someone can follow her. She'll either go home first to tell her family and then go to tell Atalanta, or she might go to Atalanta directly."

"Good. What should we have you tell her that she would be sure to pass along to Atalanta? Any suggestions?"

They thought for a while.

Artemisia had a suggestion. "Why not tell Vipsania that Judge Severus thinks that Atalanta and Pedo are alive. That would shake them up."

"Great idea. Vulso, tonight, in your pillow talk, let Vipsania know we are musing about the possibility that she and Pedo were not murdered, but are still alive. If she wants to know why, tell her the truth. Everything fits together if they are alive. But don't tell her we're acting on the theory or even believe it. Say we're just musing about it."

"I'll tell her that. I wager she'll head straight to Atalanta's hideout."

"Straton, I want you to assume one of your undercover roles and be the one to follow Vipsania when she leaves the hotel tomorrow morning."

"I look forward to doing that. I remember what she looks like from when we were at her *insula* the other day. I can dress as an ordinary plebeian, in an ordinary brown tunic, and become unnoticeable among the crowds going about every morning. I'll follow her and she'll never notice me. I'll take someone from our court with me and send him to report anything important to you while I keep watch."

"We'll be waiting with great expectations."

"You know," mused Artemisia, "if Atalanta is alive, it's almost as if you are bringing her back from the dead. She was dead when you started this investigation, and now, if your theory is correct, she's restored to life. It's almost like Orpheus and Euridice. Euridice died and Orpheus descended into the underworld, played his lyre and sang to the gods, and so got permission from the gods to bring her back to life and to lead her out of the underworld to the world above. But they warned him, if he should look back at her before they reached the upper world, she would descend back into the underworld. So Orpheus led Euridice toward the upper world, but as they neared the entrance, he could not hear her behind him and so looked back to see if she was still there. She was there, but now condemned back to the underworld.

"So maybe you should take out your lyre?" said Artemisia with a smile. "It's been a long time since you played it."

Severus looked at Artemisia. "I like that idea, *deliciae*. Tonight, I'll take out my seven-string lyre and you take out your double flute, and we'll play a duet."

"I'd love to," replied Artemisia.

And that's what they did that night, entertaining their household with a flute and lyre performance of the duet 'Orpheus and Euridice.'"

XXV

FOLLOWING VIPSANIA

That night Vulso and Vipsania had another tryst. After making love, Vulso pretended to be ready to fall asleep. Vipsania stroked him to keep him awake.

"What's going on in your investigation? Are you making any progress in finding my mother's killer?"

"No. None at all. The judge is desperate. Now that Scapula has been murdered, he doesn't even have a suspect. You want to know how desperate he is?"

She snuggled close to him.

"He's now musing about the idea that your mother is not dead at all. Can you believe that? I don't. But that's what he's thinking about."

"What makes him think that?"

"No reason. Just that he can't think of anything else. And get this, his wife Artemisia is supporting that idea. Ridiculous, of course. But that's what's going on."

"Too bad it's not true. Then my mother would still be alive. Unfortunately, I saw her dead body and was present at her cremation. So you can tell that to your judge."

"I will."

Then he closed his eyes and went to sleep, satisfied that he had planted the idea in Vipsania's mind.

Vipsania closed her eyes and tossed and turned most of the night.

At the first hour of the morning, as dawn was breaking over the City, Vipsania got out of bed, dressed, woke up Vulso, kissed him goodbye and left the hotel, heading not toward her *insula* on the Aventine Hill, but toward the center of the city and the Subura behind it.

Straton with a freedman, the former court slave Pectillus, were waiting downstairs in the hotel. Pectillus had once before worked undercover for Judge Severus, when he was investigating the case of the Persian assassin. His excellent work earned him his freedom, and as a freedman he continued working for the Court of the Urban Prefect. Now Straton selected Pectillus to work undercover with him again. At the hotel, they were both dressed inconspicuously in plain brown tunics. When Straton recognized Vipsania walking rapidly out of the hotel, the two followed at a safe distance, blending in with the crowds of people scurrying this way and that, elbow to elbow, to their morning jobs. But hiding in crowds was unnecessary. Vipsania never looked back.

They followed her, still walking rapidly, past the Circus Maximus, past the Flavian Amphitheater, skirting the Forum Romanum and the Imperial Fora, down the *Vicus Sandalarius*, then across the *Argiletum*, and into the Subura. There she strode unhesitatingly down one side street and into another until she stopped in front of a shabby *insula*. There she took a deep breath to collect herself and entered the building.

Straton spotted a taberna across the street from the *insula* and he and Pectillus went in and found a table by an open window from where they could watch the entrance to the apartment house.

"This is likely to be a lengthy wait," said Straton, "so let's have some breakfast." Straton ordered a cup of *mulsum* honey wine and a bowl of dates for himself. Pectillus also ordered *mulsum* and a soft-boiled egg with pine kernels, honey and vinegar. They then settled down to watch.

Straton nursed his food and drink, while Pectillus wolfed down his breakfast. Then Straton told him to go back to the Forum of Augustus and tell the judge where they were. Then do whatever the judge says, though I suspect he will now gather a *contubernium* of the Urban Cohort to come here ready to arrest Atalanta and Pedo.

Pectillus left and Straton sipped his wine and occasionally ate a date. While Straton appeared inconspicuous to any casual observer, his sitting by the window and looking at the *insula* across the street made him conspicuous to the waiters in the taberna. But they had already figured out without any trouble that he was a police agent of some sort watching the *insula* across the street. After a while, one waiter came up to Straton and placed some wine and water next to him, along with a bowl of fruit. "Compliments of the taberna," he said with a smile. Straton smiled back, understanding that his surveillance was understood and that he was being helped along.

A little more than an hour later, Pectillus returned and sat down at the table with Straton.

"Did you find the judge? What did he say?"

"He was in his chambers playing *latrunculi* with Alexander. I told him where we had followed Vipsania to. He asked whether we had seen Atalanta or Pedo. I told him not when I left you, but you were still watching. He told me to go back and continue the surveillance. Seeing Atalanta and Pedo alive is what he wants. It's the most important thing."

And that's what they did. A waiter brought some wine and water and a bowl of fruit for Pectillus and they drank slowly, munched sporadically, and watched constantly.

After about an hour and a half, Vipsania came out of the *insula*. She headed purposely away. "Follow her, Pectillus. I'll wait here. I think Atalanta and Pedo are probably inside. My real job is to see them alive. So I'll wait here. You stay with Vipsania."

Pectillus got up and followed her as she headed back the way she came, leaving the Subura by way of the *Argiletum*, the *Vicus Sandalarius*, skirting around the forums, passing the Flavian Amphitheater and the Circus Maximus. She even went back down Public Swimming Pool Street, but then turned down the *Vicus Portae Raudusculanae* and headed toward the Ostia Gate.

Pectillus followed, confident that he wouldn't be spotted, because Vipsania still never looked behind her.

At the Ostia Gate, Vipsania went to the area where *carpentum* coaches were parked before taking on passengers for Ostia or to travel down the Via Appia to places south of Rome. Pectillus watched her confer with a clerk by a desk and pay him some money. Obviously, she was buying passage. Obviously, then, Atalanta and Pedo were preparing to leave Rome.

When Vipsania completed her business and headed back the way she came, Pectillus went up to the clerk who had waited on Vipsania. With a tone of authority, Pectillus confronted the clerk.

"Court of the Urban Prefect. Where did that woman buy passage to?"

The clerk looked at Pectillus clad in a plain brown tunic and instantly figured out that he was surveilling that woman on a police matter and answered without objection.

"She bought passage for two on a coach leaving tomorrow morning at the 4th hour for Ostia."

"How long will it take to get there?"

"It's 18 miles between Rome and Ostia. So it should take about 4 hours."

Pectillus thanked him and left. He guessed that Vipsania would return to the *insula* that Straton was watching. Using some initiative, Pectillus headed straight to the Forum of Augustus to tell Judge Severus what he had found out.

At Severus' chambers, the judge was no longer playing *latrunculi*, but reading. Pectillus reported what he had learned at the Ostia Gate.

"The 4th hour tomorrow for Ostia," said Severus, fixing the time and place in his mind. "It looks like they're intending to take a ship somewhere.

"Good work, Pectillus. Now go back to Straton and bring him up to date. It doesn't look like Atalanta and Pedo will leave that *insula* until tomorrow. So you'll have to stay on watch overnight to be on hand first thing tomorrow morning and follow them. They'll probably hire a litter so as not to be seen on the streets."

When Pectillus left, Severus called Vulso and Crantor into his chambers, telling them what Pectillus had found out.

"I want both of you to go to Ostia today and be on hand when Atalanta and Pedo arrive there tomorrow. Follow them and find out what ship they're taking passage on. I want to know where they're intending to go. And also I want to know what other ships are leaving Ostia at around the same time, and where they are going."

"And then?" asked Vulso.

"Then report back to me."

"But doesn't that mean they may get away in the time before I return to Rome and make my report to you?"

"Not necessarily. I have something in mind. Report back to me and then I'll discuss the situation with everyone."

Meanwhile, Pectillus returned to tell Straton what had happened and what Judge Severus had told him.

"Good work, Pectillus. You were right, of course. Vipsania arrived back here a short time ago and went back into the *insula*. I guess that the judge will have the Urban Cohort waiting for them at the Ostia Gate tomorrow morning. Won't they be surprised."

Pectillus remained seated at the table while Straton took a walk around the block a few times to stretch his legs. The taberna never closed, so they stayed there all night, taking turns sleeping and watching.

The next morning, it was shortly after the 1st hour that things began to happen. Vipsania came out of the *insula* and went around the corner. She came back a little later leading a six-person litter to the front of the *insula*. Then a man and a woman came out and began to load a few musette bags into the litter. The woman carried a thin rectangular wooden case in her hand and wouldn't let go of it.

"That's them," said Straton. "I recognize Atalanta from the painting of her and the man looks like the man in the painting of Pedo, though I can't be sure from here. But I bet it's him and I bet the wooden case Atalanta is holding onto contains her painting supplies."

The man and the woman, along with Vipsania, boarded the litter and it headed out. Straton and Pectillus followed them. In Rome during the day where wheeled vehicles were prohibited, travel by foot was faster than travel by litter. So there was no trouble following behind the litter as it left the Subura and headed toward the Ostia Gate.

XXVI

A RECKONING

While following the litter with Atalanta, Pedo and Vipsania inside, along with their belongings, Straton wondered out loud where Judge Severus, Vulso and the Urban Cohort were. Were they planning to waylay the criminals somewhere along the route to the Ostia Gate or perhaps at the Ostia Gate itself, before they boarded their coach to the port of Rome? But halfway to the Ostia Gate there was still no sign of the authorities. Straton and Pectillus could do nothing but await events.

"You told the judge about their leaving Rome, didn't you?" asked Straton once more.

"I did. I told him that Vipsania bought passage for two on a coach to Ostia at the 4th hour today. He even repeated it, just to make sure he got it right."

"So where are they?"

Pectillus shrugged. "Waiting at the Ostia Gate, I suppose."

They soon arrived at the Ostia Gate, with time to spare before the 4th hour scheduled departure. The litter was directed to the place where the *carpentum* coach for Ostia was waiting. Pedo, Atalanta and Vipsania got out and began to direct slaves on the spot to put their luggage on their coach to Ostia.

Then Atalanta and Vipsania embraced and Atalanta and Pedo boarded the coach, while Vipsania waived goodbye and then left.

At the 4th hour, the coach for Ostia left Rome as scheduled. Atalanta and Pedo were on it. No one had interfered. Neither Judge Severus nor any of the Urban Cohort were on hand.

"Let's go back to the judge's chambers," said Straton, shaking his head. "I don't know what happened. Maybe there was a misunderstanding, or maybe the judge plans to intercept them in Ostia for some reason. It could be done, of course, but I don't understand. Why wait? They could have all been arrested at the Ostia Gate or even on route there. I just don't understand what's going on."

When Straton and Pectillus arrived at Judge Severus' chambers in the Forum of Augustus, they found the judge once more enrapt in a game of *latrunculi* with Alexander. But he looked up when he saw Straton and Pectillus coming in and smiled at them.

"Did they leave Rome on the 4th hour coach to Ostia?"

"Yes. Just as they were supposed to," replied Straton. "But where were you and the Urban Cohort? How come Pedo and Atalanta weren't arrested on the spot? They committed three murders, after all, Zephyrus, the charioteer and idol of the Red faction fans, and Scapula and Mucius, both members of the Senatorial Order. I don't understand why you let them go to Ostia. Are you planning to arrest them there? I just don't get it."

"I'm not planning to arrest them at all. Sit down, both of you, and I'll try to enlighten you. You were surveilling them when all of us, I mean Vulso, Flaccus, Proculus, Crantor, Alexander and Artemisia discussed what we should do.

"We had three choices. One, we could, as you expected us to do, arrest them both. What then? They would certainly be convicted of three murders and sentenced to horrible deaths in the arena. They killed, as you say, one idol of the Circus fans and two members of the Senatorial Order. And who were they? A courtesan and a shoemaker, who was also a convicted and disgraced minor official. If arrested, there would be no chance that they could avoid horrible deaths.

"However, I was not, by any stretch of the imagination, ever going to allow that ending for Atalanta. I had been appointed *iudex selectus* to find out who killed the charioteer and Atalanta and Pedo, numbers I, II and III. I was especially charged with preventing any further murders. I personally was interested in finding out who killed Atalanta because in the past she had done me a valuable service.

"But what happened? I came to this *cognitio* with a dead Atalanta. You might as well say that as a result of my solution, as Artemisia pointed out the other day, she was restored to life. So having brought her back to life, what was I supposed to do? Sentence her death? And for what? For seeking revenge against the man who raped her? In Roman law, a rapist caught in the act can be killed with no repercussions. This is a little more remote, I admit, but so what? In this case I will not countenance a death sentence for the woman who was raped."

"Didn't you even want to talk to Atalanta and tell her you were letting her go?" asked Straton.

"No. I was warned off by the story of Orpheus and Euridice. I decided not to look at Atalanta as Orpheus should not have looked back at Euridice."

"I thought you weren't superstitious."

"I'm not. But sometimes it's wiser not to take any chances."

Straton gave him a doubtful look.

"Anyway," continued the judge, "that leaves two other possibilities. If I was going to let Atalanta go, I could perhaps arrest only Pedo. He did in fact physically commit all the murders. I could put him on trial, convict him of the killings and have him thrown into the arena. But I'm faced with a not too dissimilar situation as with Atalanta. Yes, Pedo killed Scapula and Mucius, both members of the Senatorial Order. But both were criminals in their own right, guilty, though unjustly acquitted, of extorting money from the province Scapula governed as Propraetor. Also, I am mindful of Pedo's lawyer's belief that he was corrupted by Scapula, and was as much a victim of the governor's corruption as a beneficiary of it. So I'm not interested in avenging the deaths of Scapula and Mucius by killing Pedo. Maybe, as a Roman judge, I should concern myself only with the perpetrator of these murders. But I'm a retired Roman judge. And, I have to admit it, I just don't care much about the killing of criminals like Scapula and Mucius. Good riddance is my attitude.

"The third option, therefore, is not to arrest Pedo, but let him escape with Atalanta. There will be no more murders, I believe, because they've already killed the people they had a motive to kill. They can now become ordinary people in some town or other, wherever they're headed to. Atalanta can continue to paint and Pedo can even continue to be a shoemaker. That remains to be seen. But they are no longer a nemesis to anyone.

"My conclusion? I choose to let them escape from Rome. Artemisia agrees with me, as did Flaccus, Crantor and Alexander. Vulso and Proculus wanted me to at least arrest Pedo. Vulso says that the real reason I'm letting Pedo escape is because he had an astronomy diopter and a copy of Lucian's *True History* and all those astronomy books in his chest. He says I look favorably on him because of that, because he and I are interested in astronomy. Well, I don't deny that may be one factor in my decision. But not the only one. Maybe I might like Pedo, but I despise Scapula and Mucius. And also, I have to admit, I feel some sympathy for Pedo because he was corrupted by Scapula, another of his victims.

"And then again, it appears that Pedo and Atalanta belong together. They were confederates in these murders, but they are also companions and lovers. And since I'm determined to let Atalanta escape, I feel moved to let Pedo escape with her.

"I say escape, but we can also think of it in Roman law terms, as the punishment of *relegatio* -- relegation. Roman law recognizes punishments of exile to a place, like an island, which one can never leave, and relegation, from a place, like the city of Rome to which one can never return. These are legal alternatives to a death penalty, and I will not countenance a death penalty here."

Severus paused and took a drink of wine, letting his explanation sink in.

"So what do you say, Straton, and you Pectillus? What would you do?"

"Now that you've explained it," replied Straton without hesitation. "I agree with letting them escape. I mean, suffering the penalty of relegation. In fact, I applaud it."

"So do I," echoed Pectillus.

It was an easy decision for the two former slaves, Straton and Pectillus. For them, anyone who kills two corrupt Roman nobles couldn't be all bad.

"Good. I've sent Vulso and Crantor to Ostia to follow Atalanta and Pedo when they arrive and find out where they're going"

"If you're letting them escape, why do you even want to know?"

"Because I have to report to the Urban Prefect and I want to know where they went. I think I have an obligation to report this to the Prefect. When Vulso and Crantor return from Ostia, I will call everyone together and dictate a letter to the Urban Prefect telling him the solution to the case. Then I will conclude my service as Special Judge."

"There's one other matter I'm now curious about," said Straton. "What are you going to do about Novatilla and Vipsania and Heron? They all knew the body they cremated as Atalanta wasn't her and therefore conspired with Atalanta to fake her death. Don't they have some responsibility in these murders? What are you going to do about them?"

Severus thought for a moment. "I've been thinking about that. If I'm letting the chief culprits Atalanta and Pedo go with at most a penalty of relegation, I can't very well punish Atalanta's family more than that. So I suppose I should relegate them as well, but for a limited number of years rather than forever. Say five years. How does that sound?"

"Reasonable."

"Then that's what I'll do with them."

Later that afternoon, Vulso and Crantor returned from Ostia.

"Where are they going?" asked Severus.

"To Neapolis. Their ship leaves tomorrow and will arrive there in two and a half days."

"Call everyone in," said the judge. "I'll now dictate my report to the Urban Prefect."

XXVII

A LETTER TO THE URBAN PREFECT

Marcus Flavius Severus, *iudex selectus*, to Lucius Sergius Paullus, Prefect of the City of Rome, greetings:

Prefect, I am writing to you to let you know the solution to the *cognitio* you gave me to solve. I also can inform you that there will be no more murders by the perpetrators.

First, there have been three murders, not five. Those who were murdered are: victim number I, Zephyrus, the chariot driver for the Reds. Victims number V and IV were Scapula, the former governor of Bithynia and Mucius, his son-in-law, and a member of his staff in Bithynia.

As to Atalanta and Pedo, who were ostensibly victims II and III, these were faked, with already dead bodies passed off as their corpses. Rather than Atalanta and Pedo being victims, they were the perpetrators of the other three murders. Pedo physically committed each killing, but Atalanta was his co-conspirator and accomplice. How far Atalanta went along with him or provoked him, I don't know. I only know that Atalanta had a motive to kill Zephyrus because he raped her. Pedo had motives to kill Scapula and Mucius because Pedo was on the governor's staff in Bithynia and while all three were tried before the Senate for *repetundae* extortion from the province, only Pedo was convicted. Scapula, the most culpable of all, was acquitted along with his son-in-law Mucius. Presumably, the fact that they were members of the Senatorial Order, while Pedo was not even an *honestior,* just a lower class *humilior*, could have had some importance in the minds of the senators judging his case.

In any event, the victims were all victims of revenge. This was the motive that provoked both Atalanta and Pedo. Like the goddess Nemesis avenging injustice with her dagger. Since they have killed all the people they wanted to kill, I can conclude with certainty that there will be no more murders by them. And since Zephyrus was killed because he raped Atalanta, no other chariot drivers will be targets of these perpetrators.

As for Atalanta and Pedo, they have fled Rome. I was able to trace them to Ostia where they boarded ship for Neapolis. Whether they intend to remain there or go from Neapolis somewhere else I do not know. Neapolis is outside the 100-mile jurisdiction of the Prefect of Rome, so I did not go further in investigating them there.

Therefore, as a Roman judge endowed under Roman law with far-reaching discretion, I find Atalanta and Pedo guilty of murder and, because of extenuating circumstances, impose the penalty of *relegatio* from Rome for life. The accomplices from Atalanta's family, her mother Novatilla, her daughter Vipsania and her bodyguard Heron, I will sentence to *relegatio* from Rome, but for a term of 5 years rather than for life. This is because they conspired with Atalanta to fake her death, but I have no evidence that they were aware of or took part in any of the murders Atalanta and Pedo committed.

One final note, Prefect. I intend to impose these verdicts and sentences in an informal manner rather than holding a trial in court of any of these defendants. Such a trial will certainly become public knowledge and evoke calls for drastic punishments because of the victims, one sports hero and two members of the Senatorial Order. I do not want this to happen. Therefore, I will call Atalanta's family into my chambers and inform them of my findings and sentences. They will be ordered to leave the City for five years and will be instructed to communicate to Atalanta her and Pedo's lifetime *relegatio*. All will assuredly accept this result without further court proceedings.

Vale.

/seal/ Marcus Flavius Severus

Severus gave a big smile.

"After settling the case with Atalanta's family in my chambers tomorrow, I'm going to head to my retirement villa in the Alban Hills

"So as of tomorrow then, the case is closed."

HISTORICAL NOTE

The racing career of Zephyrus closely tracks the recorded statistics of the famous driver Crescens. See *Corpus Inscriptionum Latinarum* 6.10050; ILS 5285. The four factions in the Roman Circus were the Reds (*Russata*), Greens (*Praesina*), Blues (*Veneti*) and Whites (*Albata*).

The Seneca quote about children and adults playing the game of magistrates is at *de Constantia,* 2.3-3.

The books of Pliny's Natural History about painting and painters are NH XXXIII - XXXV

Trials before the Senate are discussed in detail in Talbert, Richard, J. A., *The Senate of Imperial Rome,* (Princeton U. Press, 1984), ch. XVI, The senatorial court, pp. 460-487; Garnsey, Peter, *Social Stratus and Legal Privilege in the Roman Empire* (Oxford, 1970) ch.2, The senatorial court from the Flavians to the Severans, pp.43-64.

Pertinax later became Emperor in March 190, succeeding Commodus after he was assassinated. Pertinax was the first son of a slave to become Emperor. He was assassinated by the Praetorian Guard 3 months later, but his memory was honored and he was deified during the reign of Septimius Severus.

The recipes at the Symposium in chapter XIII and throughout come from the Roman cookbook, *De re coquinaria*, (*The Art of Cooking*) by Apicius, the 1st century Roman gourmet, translated by Flower and Rosenbaum, *The Roman Cookery Book* (Peter Nevill Ltd., London and New York, 1958).

About the game of *Latrunculi*, it was the closest game the Romans had to chess or Go, games of pure thought, without dice. I've discussed it fully in the historical note to "*The Return of Spartacus,*" pp. 236-7.

The cover image is from an Athenian amphora of the 5th century BCE, depicting the goddess Nemesis pointing out a transgressor to Tyche, the goddess the Romans called Fortuna. Nemesis was essentially the goddess of vengeance and retribution, particularly against perpetrators of crime. The story recorded on the amphora is that Nemesis is the mother of Helen of Troy and points her out when she was having an affair with Paris, a transgression leading to the Trojan war and all its dire consequences.

Finally, I once again wish to express my gratitude and love to Ruth Chevion not only for her careful editing and many insightful suggestions, but most importantly for her personal and loving support and care over many years.